isoo's diary

First published in 04. 10. 2024
Design   Joen isoo
writer   Joen isoo
Instagram @jeon2soo
           @gallery_walkingwolves

Copyright © 2024 Jeon ISoo

ISBN   979-11-94085-12-6 (03810)

Published by PNPBOOK
16, Shinchon-ro, Paku-si, Gyeonggi-do, 10880

Hermonhouse is an imprint of PNPBOOK

isoo's diary

1

CONTENTS

2018

Sickness 12

Greed 14

A Rainy Day 16

After Watching the Film Billy Elliot 18

I'm Going to Grow Old in Style 19

The Meaning of Possession 22

I Can't See My Own Flaws, but I Can See
Others' Flaws All Too Well 24

To Become Happy means 28

Wootae's Tears 30

The Sounds of Life 34

Reading Other People 38

Our Language 40

Merry Christmas 43

Being Strong 46

Getting a Delivery 50

2019

The Tree inside My Heart 54

Are You Still Sad? 57

Could Anything Be More Important Than People? 60

A Small Change of Heart 62

The Ability to Look Around and Think of Other People 68

Too Much Sweetness Will Rot Your Teeth 74

My mom 79

During the Fight 83

A flower floats up 86

About the Feeling of Anger 90

No Two Things Are Exactly the Same 94

At the front of the Rabu inn 96

Yudam's Sobs 98

The Old Woman at the Five-Day Market 106

A little myself 112

The Real Me 116

Words That Lift Our Spirits 118

Saying Nice Things I Didn't Really Mean 120

Becoming Free 124

How Many Wounds Did It Carry? 126

I Walk to Clear My Mind 130

Showing You Care 132

What do you think about 134

If Food Fell from Heaven 138

Too Much Talk Will Tie Yourself 140

If I Could Only Live to the Age of 20 144

2020

A World of Your Own 148

If I Were in Her Shoes 150

Something Exciting 154

I have a lot on my mind 158

To Mom 2 162

To Mom 3 164

A Present for Children's Day 168

Half of the World Is Starving 170

Those Who Are Dear to Me 172

Yudam's Lies 178

To Mom 4 186

Call me "Hyung" 190

What Do We Do About Yudam? 194

This Much Is Enough! 202

Wounded Feelings 205

I Am Happy 210

People Who Show You What Happiness Is 212

I Am Who I Am 218

Santa Claus 220

2018

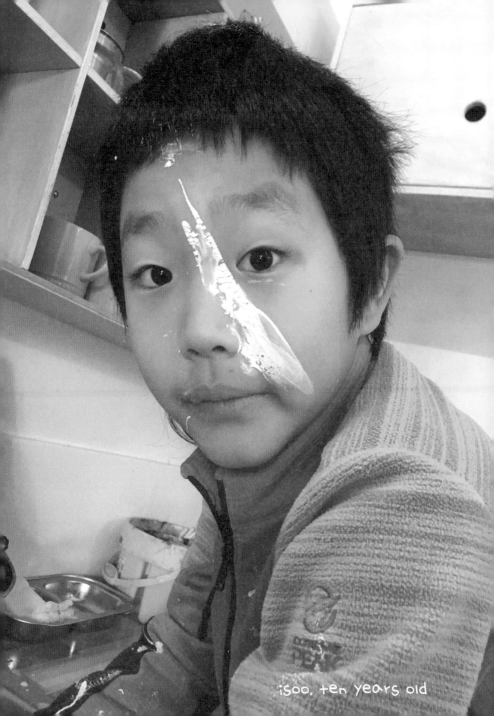

isoo, ten years old

Sickness

One day, Mom got sick and went to the doctor.

When the doctor tersely asked her what was wrong, she started to go into the details of where she was hurting, how long she had been hurting, and various contributing factors. But then, the doctor cut her off and said, "Just tell me where it hurts!" Mom's feelings must have become hurt then, too.

What if the doctor had listened carefully to his patient and said, "You can get better, you'll be okay"? It seems to me the first step in treating a patient should be giving them hope. I wonder how many doctors actually heed what their patients say or pay attention to how they feel. Sick people go to the doctor with the hope that they'll get better. They want to hear encouraging words; they want to hear that they can recover.

Sickness... Having been sick before probably gives you a better understanding of other people's sickness. I think a doctor ought to be able to treat sick people's hearts before attending to their bodies.

I want to send a message of hope to everyone who is sick: It's going to be okay! You'll get better soon.

Greed

Right now, what I'm thinking about is greed.

When people are greedy, I think their greed causes them to forfeit even what they have. Being generous to others can be a kind of greed, too, if your heart isn't in it.

If you let greed push you to recklessly pursue whatever it is that you want right now, you'll end up exhausted, like swimming against a current. But if you just go with the flow, the current will naturally take you where you want to go.

I think that's how life works, too. If you keep your feelings flexible, I think you'll get to feel everything you want in life. But first, stop being greedy...

Rainy day

The sky is crying. It's a long, ugly cry. But I think it's crying for a reason. There was a huge downpour on the day the Sewol ferry went down, too.

Does the sky know it all? Does it know how so many people hurt so badly, how they shed so many tears? I cried a lot myself on that day. That's why I think the sky is crying for a reason. The rain was unusually heavy on that day, too, just as it is now...

I wish that I could turn back time to Mom's childhood, just once. Mom told me that no one talked about the dust particles in the air back then. She said kids could frolic in unpolluted ponds, rivers, and meadows, as well as in fields in the rain. Now the meadows I could have romped in are paved over and covered by tall apartments and office buildings, while the ponds, rivers and even the ocean are covered with green rot.

That's not how it's supposed to be, and the very thought brings tears to my eyes.

Does the sky have a reason for crying, too? Let's cry together. Let it all out. I just wish all this rain could wash everything clean.

After watching Billy Elliot

Date: October 18, 2018

When Billy made up his mind to do ballet and gained the courage to take responsibility for what he said, his diligence and determination struck me as things I ought to learn. Billy gave me a lot to think about.

I was most impressed by the scene in which Billy responded with action, not nasty words, when his dad got angry at him for pursuing ballet even after being told to stop. Billy's courageous actions invigorated me.

In the movie, Billy's dad believes in the stereotypes that boys ought to play football or do boxing or wrestling, and that ballet is something that little girls do. I was very impressed to see the dad's stereotypes changing due to Billy's determination. I was moved when the dad came to respect Billy's opinions and make sacrifices so his son's dream could come true.

I think that must have made Billy happy. It's nice to think my own dad could do the same thing.

I want to become a cool old person

Date: October 25, 2018

When I watched the film [Young@Heart], it had a lot to say to me. The film was surprising and touching from beginning to end. It was remarkable to see the choir of old people in their 70s and 80s singing and practicing for a big concert. It was also sad when Bob, who had been so determined to put on the show, passed away during a rehearsal. In one scene, he had promised to take the stage while looking at a concert poster.

Then there was Joe, who still managed to crack jokes with the nurse even after being diagnosed with the cancer he'd been dreading. He told the nurse he wasn't afraid of death since he'd done everything he wanted to do with his life. That line got me thinking that maybe people are afraid of dying because they haven't gotten to do what they really want. I realized that I should do the things I really want to do, just as Joe did...

Fred, who had trouble breathing and had to carry around an oxygen bag, had such a wonderful voice.

One of the women in the movie told her friends to keep practicing and not be sad when she died since she was going to sit on a rainbow to watch them instead of going up to heaven.

The smiling faces and twinkling eyes of the old men and women singing their hearts out on the day of the concert were more amazing and beautiful than any singers I had ever seen. I can say for certain that such beauty can only be conveyed by voices that have grown mature over the long years of the singers' lives.

I want to mirror the passion in their voices. That's something I want to learn. I love those people.

Thank you. I hope to remember the mature voices of all those old men and women who taught me something so meaningful.

To possess something

Sometimes I become fixated on something and get the sudden urge to have it for my own. I'll crave one thing after another, convinced I can't relax until they're in my hands. Eventually, calm will return. After a while, I'll look back at my behavior and wonder why I behaved like that.

I think love works the same way. Sometimes you only feel secure when you're with the person you love. That's why I couldn't let go of Mom for 10 years.

Looking back now, it wasn't until Mom started having occasional bouts with illness that I realized her peace of mind was more important than mine. I realized that Mom was bothered by all the niggling pains that she'd been concealing and suppressing for 10 years. I feel that if you love someone, you need to know how to let them go.

Even when Mom took a vacation, a couple of days was hardly enough time to cure ailments that had been a decade in the making.

Mom was sick again today, and I was, too.

She told me it's really important that we all love everyone, not just people we think are special, and that we tell each other we love them.

I respect what Mom told me.

She's my closest friend and very dear to me.

What I feel now is the need to practice letting go of my selfish desire to possess her.

I love Mom, and I want to say this to everyone: Thank you, I love you!

I Can't See My Own Flaws, but I Can See Others' Flaws All Too Well

Date: November 8, 2018

I took an image of myself out of my heart and placed it down before me. That's the only way I can get a good look at myself.

When I woke up this morning, I scolded my siblings for crying because Mom wasn't there beside them. When they griped about their breakfast, I told them to just eat what's on their plate, and when they got cranky, I told them to hush. In all honesty, it's hard to imagine what I looked like during all of that. I doubt I looked very nice. My siblings must all have had their reasons for acting like that. I guess all that crying, griping, and crankiness made me lose my cool.

Mom doesn't scold us, push us to do anything, or order us around. After a few minutes, she told me I used to be just like my siblings are and asked me to be a little patient with them.

Come to think of it, I sometimes get teary-eyed when Mom isn't next to me in the morning, I've been known to gripe about food I don't want to eat, and there are times when I feel cranky for no good reason. Whenever that happens, Mom doesn't get as impatient as I did with my siblings today. The first thing Mom always does is try to understand how other people are feeling.

Sometimes I stick my nose into other people's business without even realizing what I'm doing. So here's what I'll tell myself today: "People have reasons for what they do. That might feel frustrating, but I've got to be patient with them. After all, I used to be the same way!"

At the artist's room

To become happy means

I'd had a dream.

There was a long dark room.

There was nothing in it aside from a single light.

The light roamed around the room, and I moved with it, trying to seize it. When I caught the light in my hand, I took a peep inside.

It was a firefly!

That put me in a fantastic mood.

That was happiness, I felt.

That happiness was still with me when I woke up. I'm going to seize this moment just as I seized that light.

When the warm sunlight shines upon me, I'm happy.

It seems to give me the strength to start the day.

When I get up, Mom is the first one to greet me.

"Did you sleep well? Let's have another happy day today. Be strong!"

Along with that greeting, she gives me a smile.

Wrapped in her smile, it's not hard to become happy.

I don't want to miss a single moment because I know that's what happiness is.

At last, the day has begun.

Today is going to be another interesting day.

It's going to be a happy day.

Just thinking so makes it actually happen!

Wootae's tears

November 19 is the day when my younger brother, Wootae, was born. Our plan was to go to a restaurant over an hour away to have steak, which he had been looking forward to for a long time. To be honest, I was probably looking forward to it even more than him. I wanted to eat steak, too.

Wootae told me he remembered how delicious the steak had been at that restaurant two years ago. That's why he'd been saving this visit for his birthday. Full of anticipation, he hummed with excitement the whole way to the restaurant. I felt the same way.

When we finally got to the restaurant, Wootae and I hurried to the entrance and slipped inside the door. But just then a lady told us we couldn't come in. I didn't understand. When Wootae didn't move, she pushed him toward the door and said, "You're not allowed inside."

So when I said, "We came to eat here," she replied, "This is a no-kids zone."

"What is that?"

"It means that kids aren't allowed inside," she said.

That didn't make any sense to me. "I told you, we're here for a meal. Today is my brother's birthday!"

But the lady repeated herself angrily.

"You can't come in here! Get a move on!"

My mood soured, and Wootae slowly moved toward the door, disappointment clear on his face. Once we were outside, I saw tears streaming down his cheeks.

Just then, Mom came up and saw that Wootae was crying. When I told Mom we weren't allowed into the restaurant, she said, "That can't be right! We all came together last time." Mom stepped inside and was in there for a while. When she came out, she said, "I don't think we can eat here. Let's go somewhere else. Wootae, the chef here apparently had ear surgery and needs things to be quiet until his ears get better."

Let's try to be understanding."

I could read the expression on Mom's face.
Wootae's sadness was hard for both of us to bear.
Wootae cried the whole way back.
"I just wanted to eat! We could have eaten without saying a thing," he said. As Mom quietly held Wootae in her arms, her eyes were full of sadness, too.

I understand that grown-ups want to enjoy a quiet meal and that they can't do that if there are kids around. But I think that kids' right to enter a business should outweigh grown-ups' right to relax. All kids will grow up someday, after all. Grown-ups seem to forget they used to be kids.

I was reminded of what the boy asks his father in <Life Is Beautiful>, a movie I watched a while ago: "Why aren't Jews or dogs allowed to go in?"

Grown-ups seem to forget they used to be kids.

The sounds of life

Date: December 5, 2018

My eyes opened early in the morning. But when I looked outside, it was still dark. Having woken up so early, I felt a sudden urge to get up and go for a walk. I quietly opened the door and went outside. Sitting on the doorstep, I put on one shoe and then the other, then walked out the gate...

How refreshing the early morning air was.

I began to walk. After a while, I saw an old woman sweeping the street. For some reason, her broom sounded very loud.

Then a big vehicle drove up, and some men got out, diligently picking up the trash and moving it around. They grunted with the effort, making a huge racket.

I kept walking until I reached an underpass. I saw a figure lying on the stairs beneath it, head down, body hunched over and trembling all over.

My heart ached with the thought that this person had spent the whole night there.

I kept walking without a break.

But then heat suddenly swept over me, a heat that was almost unbearable. Dust swirled around me, and I could barely open my eyes.

Gradually, a large number of children became visible to me. In their eyes, there was a desperation I had never known. They were too hungry to even cry, but their breathing was very loud in my ears.

I looked behind me again. I was in a place that was full of noise and movement, with lots of people among the tall buildings. Some people were carrying around very heavy burdens, others were driving motorcycles to deliver newspapers in the early morning hours, and still others were shouting as they hawked their wares. As they all rushed about their lives, the sound of sweat dripping from their bodies was very loud.

I escaped that place and began walking again.

I kept going until I came to the bottom of a very high mountain.

Below a rickety roof, an old man was alone, tiredly spooning rice from a bowl. His only side dishes were a piece of kimchi and a dish of soy sauce. With each spoonful, the man was swallowing the sorrows of the long years of his life. He also seemed to be eagerly waiting for someone. When I slowly approached him and reached out my hand... my eyes opened.

It had been a dream.

I found myself thinking that we ought to share with the people around us and take care of them...

How many of us truly care about or pay attention to the sounds of the lives of the many people around us? I vowed not to forget about the important sounds of life and the tiny sounds that I typically don't notice.

Noonchi
(Reading Other People)

Date: December 12, 2018

An older boy I know is always trying to read other people. I suppose that's because he's often been told he's not very observant. He gets scolded for butting in when visitors are over and for talking back to his elders.

Over time, the boy's eyes have gotten busier. He's gotten into the habit of glancing around in all directions. Sometimes he'll say he's busy when he's just sitting there, doing nothing at all.

I got curious about why the boy's eyes were always in motion and started paying closer attention to him when he came over to our house.

One day, I saw the boy hiding a snack behind his back after his mom told him to stop eating. When she would tell him he was getting fat, he would bend over to hide his belly, and I realized he'd developed a habit of hunching his shoulders. And when she told him to stop walking like that, he started looking down at his feet, too. All that pressure from his mom was shaping his body, or rather, his habits.

The boy told me his mom had told him to study thousands of times and that he wished he could go the rest of his life without studying. What could have made him hate studying? He said the mere sight of a textbook was enough to irritate him. He would sit at his desk with a book open and steal a glance at me and then at his mom. When she told him to hurry up, he would immediately bury his head in the book.

When he gets scolded for saying the slightest thing wrong, tears well up in his eyes. So, he tries to read the people around him. He tries to guess how they'll react to what he wants to say and the places he wants to go.

You ought to feel confident doing what you want to do and saying what you want to say, regardless of how other people will respond. Whatever the situation, isn't it more important to look into your heart than to worry about what other people will say?

These were the thoughts I wanted to write about today. I ought to think about whether I'm too worried about what other will people think of me, too.

Our language

Date: December 19, 2018

We kids have our own world and our own language. But grown-ups have apparently forgotten the language of kids.

Grown-ups used to be kids, too. To understand our language, they first have to be able to know what we're feeling. That's why you need to translate the words that people say into the language of the heart.

Sometimes, I serve as the translator in our house. This all started one day when I got mad at my youngest sibling, Yudam, when she was throwing a tantrum. I shouted at her to stop. Then Mom told me that when Yudam was throwing a tantrum, she was actually saying, "Hug me," and when she threatened to leave the house, she was actually saying, "I'm angry."

That's when I realized that I'd been wrong. It turns out that grown-ups aren't the only ones who don't know the language of the heart...

When grown-ups get irritated with us kids, they often say, "What's the matter?" "What's wrong with you?" "You're frustrating me!" and "Spit it out!" Instead of saying what is actually inside, we just wait for them to translate our words.

Whenever my little sister Yudam gets angry or stubborn, I try to remember what Mom told me. If I translate her words, I can tell that she probably means, "Mom! Hug me, pay attention to me, be nice to me!"

Whenever my younger siblings Wootae, Yudam, and Yujeong are unhappy with something, they run and tell Mom. What they're trying to say is "Mom! This is what I don't like. Please pay attention to my feelings!"

When my younger siblings get into a fight, I sometimes translate for them. When I listen to my siblings or even my friends, I've begun to hear what they say in translation. This is one of the ways in which I'm changing.

The best part of all of this is that I've gotten more relaxed. When people feel relaxed, their words become kinder, too.

Mom tells me she used to be a kid just like me. I'm thankful that Mom is a grown-up who knows these things and can look after us. When I grow up, I won't forget the language of the heart that kids use to express themselves, just like Mom. That's the kind of dad I'm going to be.

Merry Christmas

Date: October 25, 2018

Whenever Christmas comes around, I feel warm inside. The snow drifting down from the sky stirs up my emotions. Christmas is a day when everyone seems to become a little kinder.

There's a scene about Christmas in the book Little Women. I can picture the girls marching across the white snow, carrying a tablecloth and a breakfast basket as a gift for the poor old woman next door. In my mind, they all look happy, even though they're skipping their own breakfast.

The present this book gave me is the warmth you get when you give up your possessions for someone else, even if they don't make a fancy present.

While there are 365 days in the year, I think Christmas is probably the hottest of them all. While the world is blanketed in cold snow, our hearts are warmer than they are at any other time.

There are times when everything you see just looks wonderful. I think that everyone must feel that way on Christmas. It's a day when even people who don't usually greet you say, "Merry Christmas."

I really love the feeling of being greeted by strangers.

That's why my spirts lift as Christmas draws near.

I'm so excited today.

That's because it's December 25, Christmas Day.

Hooray!

Christmas is probably the hottest of them all,
while the world is blanketed in cold snow.

Being Strong

Date: December 29, 2018

What does it mean to be strong? I'm reminded of fables that Mom read me when I was little. One was about a mouse who gave some unexpected help to a mighty lion. Another was about a vain wolf who thought himself to be the strongest animal in the world. And there was another about a fox who was so clever that he managed to steal a meaty bone from a dog.

While I was listening to those fables, I found myself thinking that even strength and intelligence can turn ugly when they're put to selfish use. That's not the way such strength is supposed to be used. Today, I learned I'm not that strong.

According to Dad, my little sister Yujeong has a somewhat different concept of time from other children. Because of that, we find her very frustrating. She has trouble understanding things that seem obvious to us and drives us crazy by staring and pestering and nagging us to do things we thought she already knew how to do.

She's much slower than us, which often makes things hard on Mom.

I took Yujeong on a walk along with my younger brother Wootae, my other younger sister Yudam, and our dog Toto. We were standing there by the street, waiting for some cars to go by, when Yujeong tried to run into the street, even though I'd told her not to several times.

A guy in a car rolled down his window and yelled at us. When Yujeong acted up yet again, he shouted, "Are you stupid? Why do you keep running into the street?" I apologized to him, but he said, "Just look after your stupid little sister!"

At that, Wootae shouted, "My little sister isn't stupid!" and flung the grass and flowers he was carrying at the car. The man jumped out of his car and stormed over toward us, shouting all the while. Wootae stood tall in front of Yujeong, glaring at the man. I couldn't say a thing.

After it was all over, Wootae said, "You must be stupid, Isoo! Why didn't you say anything?"

I thought it over when I got home. True strength, it seems to me, doesn't mean being strong the way most people think. Rather, it means using the strength you have in the right way. When I saw Wootae standing up to that buff-looking guy to protect our weak little sister, several ideas passed through my mind. In the future, I mean to work on my strength of mind so that I can encourage others and set a good example myself...

Today, I learned how to look into my heart with a little more courage.

In my opinion, a strong person is one who treats weaker people with gentleness and humility while standing up to stronger people on behalf of the weaker ones. Just like Mom, and just like Wootae today...

True strength doesn't mean being strong the way
most people think. It means using the strength you
have in the right way.

Getting a Delivery

My siblings and I like getting deliveries.

When someone hands us a package, it feels just like getting a present, whatever may actually be inside.

Whenever the delivery man comes to our house, we sprint outside, racing each other at full tilt to collect the package.

Then we squabble to tear it open. Watching the scene, the delivery man can't help but laugh.

One day, I heard the gruff voice of the delivery man and rushed outside - only to find Wootae standing there alone.

For reasons of his own, he held out an empty box and said, "You have a delivery."

"Stop teasing me. You had me totally fooled! I thought it was an actual delivery."

"Isoo, I really enjoy it when we get deliveries! I wanted to share that joy with other people," he told me.

Since then, Wootae's dream has been to become a delivery person. He began to practice saying the phrase "You have a delivery" every day and even started mumbling it in his sleep. I think he might actually become a delivery person.

Wootae says that just as getting deliveries makes us happy, bringing happiness to other people makes him happy. That's why it also made me happy when Wootae said he will become a delivery person.

I hope Wootae will be able to deliver his feelings to other people, just as the clouds bring the rain and snow.

I like having this kind of brother. I like the kind of person he is.

2019

Isoo, 11 years old

The Tree inside My Heart

Date: January 3, 2019

I'm always happy when I get up in the morning. Every morning, Mom says to me, "Did you sleep well? Let's have another happy day today."

From that humble place, the tree of happiness in my heart stretches out its strong branches once again today. There hasn't been a single day in my life when the leaves of happiness haven't rustled on that tree.

I sometimes get sad or angry, but my family always brings me strength. They make it possible to always keep the hope of happiness in my heart even when I'm sad or angry. That's how I'm always able to laugh.

Happiness is always there for us all.

But some people chase after happiness as if it were very far away.

I like feeling refreshed in the morning. And I'm happy because of the time I'm given, because I get to write like this, because we have food to eat, because I have somewhere warm to sleep, and because there are people thinking of me.

From that perspective, there are many things to be happy about and to be thankful for. Sometimes I run into people who say they aren't happy. But it seems to me they're only unhappy because they think they are.

Perhaps they think they're unhappy because things aren't going their way. If you think about it, when things do go our way, we tend to take it for granted instead of being happy about it. However, when things don't go our way, we tend to complain.

I think we should take the opposite approach. When things go our way, we should be happy, and when things don't go our way, we should put them out of our mind for a while. Adjusting our attitude like that should make us happier.

I think we should cultivate a great big tree of happiness in our hearts, a tree that extends its branches to the sky as tender green leaves slowly sprout on each branch. I think that happiness exists inside us. I hope that today will be a happy day for us all.

Are You Still Sad?

Date: January 14, 2019

My notebook disappeared - the one I'd been recording my ideas in for so long. Someone must have gotten into the box where I'd always kept it. I'd hidden it away so carefully, so how could it be gone? In shock, I began to ransack the house.

I shouted at Mom, at Wootae, and at my other siblings, asking them if they'd seen my notebook. My sudden shrieks had them staring at me wide-eyed. The urge to find the notebook blocked out all other thoughts, and I have no idea what I was blabbering.

As I rushed past the woodworking shop, I thought I caught a glimpse of someone inside. Scurrying back, I peeked into the room and saw Yujeong sitting at the desk, busily coloring something. With a sinking feeling, I went over and looked at what she was working on.

It was my notebook. She'd dribbled carpenter glue on it, coated it with dust, cut it up with scissors, and frayed the cover with what seemed to be sandpaper.

I burst into tears.

Right now, I'm holding that notebook.

My heart aches and stings as if it has been rubbed with sandpaper, too. Even the pictures I'd drawn for my first book, A Little Alligator Taco, are gone beneath the black squiggles that Yujeong drew with black pastel crayons...

It feels awful to lose all my new ideas from the past year like this.

Through lunch and even after dinner, a cloud has hung over my heart today. A drizzle is still coming down.

I'm trying to comfort myself with the thought that many other people probably feel this way when they lose a notebook.

We need to be careful with people's feelings because hurt feelings last a long time. I think it's really hard to heal those wounds. I'm still in the fog right now, and I can't see my joy.

I can't even tell if it's nearby or far away - my joy is lost in the fog. I don't know when it will come back to me. Even so, the reason I'm still sad is because I haven't let go of the notebook in my heart. Even joy seems to move further away because of this.

Could Anything Be More Important Than People?

Date: January 15, 2019

I don't think anything is more important than people. Today was a valuable day for me because I learned something important. I learned that being overwhelmed by endless suffering is just a stage of growth; in fact, it's my friend.

I hope to learn a lot from my little sister Yujeong about a weakness of mine that I keep struggling with. When I scold her or say mean things to her, she gets sad, but when I smile and call her name, it takes less than five seconds for her to put all of that out of her head and start giggling again. It's really amazing. Yujeong may be smaller than others her age, but in this respect, she's bigger than us all.

I don't want to stay sad forever. Soon enough, I'll be back on my feet and back in the race. Someday, I'll learn that the sadness I feel right now isn't a big deal.

Despite knowing all that, I'm still stuck in this cycle. But if anything has changed, it's that I'm figuring things out faster than I used to. I've still got a long way to go, but I think I've earned a pat on the back.

Yujeong has already forgotten everything. I'd better play with her today.

Just like Newton's first law of motion, the joy of the morning remains in motion until someone gets in the way. That's how we are happy. That's how Yujeong and I are happy.

A Small Change of Heart

At some point today, Yudam's whiny voice and griping started to get on my nerves. When I could no longer hold back the anger bubbling up inside of me, I went over to Mom.

"I don't know why Yudam gripes about things that are no big deal. I wish she wouldn't do that!" I complained.

I'd thought that Mom would feel the same way as me, but her response was different than I expected. "Rather than assuming that Yudam is to blame, perhaps we should think about whether we made her act like that."

That made me seriously reflect upon how I'd treated Yudam. Looking back, I recalled the things I'd done to her: pushing her away when I was busy with my work, playing soccer with Wootae instead of playing princess with her, not keeping my promises to play with her later, and getting mad at her for always falling over and getting in the way when I let her join our games.

Thinking it over, I guess that Yudam must have gotten pretty lonely. I realized she might be throwing tantrums to get our attention, and that she might be redirecting her desire for love into her desire for things.

"Mom, if we were the ones who made Yudam that way, I think we ought to set her right again," I said. She gave me a smile and pulled me in for a hug.

Changing my attitude set my mind at ease. When Yudam was being cranky, I went up to her with a smile.

"Hey, Yudam. It's been a while since we've done anything exciting. Do you want to play with me?"

Just getting a little attention seems to be enough to delight Yudam. All I did was talk with her and run around in circles in the yard, but she said she really liked me and started sharing the cookies, candy, and gummy treats she'd been saving up.

Yudam ran over to Mom and said, "I really like my big brother Isoo! As long as I have him, I don't need anything else."

My small change of heart changed the way Yudam felt and made me feel warm inside, too. Seeing Yudam so happy made me wonder why I'd ignored her for so long. I'd just assumed that she had a problem, not knowing that we were the cause. We'd almost turned Yudam's kind and lovely heart into something mean and ugly.

People instinctively try to protect themselves by camouflaging the pieces of their heart in the many colors of a chameleon, to keep others from recognizing their feelings. But if you take a closer look - if you look for those feelings as you would search for something in a hidden picture puzzle - they can definitely be seen.

I had failed to recognize Yudam's feelings before, but now I can definitely see them. If I say something nice to Yudam, she'll smile and say something nice back to me. And if I respond nicely to something mean she says to me, she'll soon put aside her mean words. Since I was the one who dug that lonely hole in Yudam's heart, I'm going to fill it in again.

One thing that Yudam helped me learn today is that warm and cheerful words are stronger than any words of anger, no matter how dark and powerful.

I think that love has always been in our hearts, since they were first made.

My song
〈we all love Sunday〉

The Ability to Look Around and Think of Other People

Date: February 27, 2019

My maternal grandfather is very kind, a perfect gentleman. At first glance, he might look a little intimidating, with his leathery skin, sharp eyes, and angular features. But I've known Grandpa since I was born, which I guess has taught me that you can't judge a book by its cover.

Grandpa is always busy.

At home, he seems to have more to do than Grandma.

His hands are always in motion. When he gets home, he'll start up the rice cooker and do the dishes. Whenever I look up, he seems to be ironing the clothes, hanging up the laundry, watering the plants, or cooking up some buchimgae (savory pancakes) if we want something to eat. Grandpa hardly ever seems to slow down. He even fixed a meal for his own birthday, horrifying Mom and Grandma. But when they objected, he just said, "Goodness, does it matter who fixes the meal? What matters is that we eat together."

Somehow, I've gotten used to Grandpa's way of doing things. When he comes down to Jeju Island to visit us, he'll start doing housework as soon as he takes off his shoes. He'll do the dishes, fix a meal, and clean the house even when Mom says he doesn't need to. He'll also sit down for a game of "air" with me and my siblings when we ask him to, or play "barley, barley, rice" with a smile as long as Yudam wants. Surely Grandpa must feel a little put upon, but he's always full of laughter.

On the last day of his visit, Grandpa was roving around the house, looking for chores he could take care of. When Mom suggested that he take a break, he came up with the following response.

"After I'm gone, you'll be left to shoulder this whole burden by yourself! For as long as I'm here, you're the one who needs to take a break. I'll take care of it, so you just sit back and relax!"

Grandpa's words kept playing through my mind as we were driving him to the airport. His words made it clear how much he thinks of Mom.

When Mom was putting me to bed that night, she told me a story from when I was a baby. When Grandpa came over to our house, he would wash my cloth diapers and neatly fold them up once they were dry. He would feed me, carry me around on his back, and cradle me in his arms. He wanted to give Mom a few days of peace, so he would change my diaper when I woke up early in the morning. When I went number two, he would mix some hot water he'd boiled in the kettle into cold water in a basin until he got the right temperature and wash my bottom, then carry me around and sing me to sleep. Grandpa had been a smoker for more than 40 years until the day I pushed away from a hug because of the nasty cigarette smell. That made him very sad, and he quit smoking that very day. More than a decade has gone by since his last smoke.

I don't remember any of that, but my heart melts whenever I see Grandpa. Through his actions, he has taught me that other people's joy can make us happier than our own. He has taught me that instead of complaining about someone else not doing their fair share, it's more important that everyone is happy, regardless of who works the hardest.

I think that when we recognize that other people are struggling and try to take on some of their burden, we can all experience joy. One person's thoughtfulness is what made possible the greater love that's now being passed down to us. I feel that this is what makes us truly happy, and that's why I like Grandpa so much.

Grandpa has shown me a more profound kind of love. As long as you have love, there's no reason to feel discontented, even if life is a little tougher or you don't have as many things.

I guess I understand how Mom can say that just watching me eat makes her feel full, how she doesn't begrudge giving up everything, how she can laugh and says she's fine even when she's tired - it's because she looks at everything through the eyes of love, without any second thoughts. It's because her heart is filled with a warmth greater than the joy that comes from having things.

If everyone were to share their warmth with just one other person, the world would surely soon be full of warm-hearted people.

I miss Grandpa so much today. Soon, I'll be going to see him. I hope I'm able to still see him even when I'm as big as Dad. I hope Grandpa will stick around for me and stay in good health... that way I'll have a chance to carry him around and fix a meal for him, too...

If everyone were to share their warmth with just one other person, the world would surely soon be full of warm-hearted people.

Too Much Sweets Will Rot Your Teeth

Date: March 17, 2019

I hear a lot about video games nowadays. Some other kids' mothers have asked Mom what to do about video games and how long kids should be allowed to play. Mom has shared her opinion about games, but I guess my own opinion goes something like this.

Games as I see them are a kind of family activity. We play Chinese checkers, Korean chess, Western chess, and soccer together. We also go bowling or go to the youth center to play the car driving game there. When we're waiting at the theater before a movie, I'll play the coin-operated airplane game with Mom or air hockey with Wootae. Sometimes my whole family will play basketball, three on three.

But when it comes to my friends, they often do things by themselves on the computer. They talk about how they can't get a game out of their head even when they're eating with their family or studying at school.

When I stop by a cafe or take the subway on a trip to Seoul, lots of people around me are generally in the middle of some complicated game on their phone. Sometimes, I find myself looking down at their phone screens. And when I'm at school, I see older kids playing games on the computer and hear my friends talking about how they only get to play games for a few hours at home and wish they could play all night long.

Considering how badly those kids always want to play video games, I figure they must be really fun.

The year before last, I heard the following story from a teacher at the alternative school I was attending. "For a long time, I used to be obsessed with gaming. More than four years have passed since I quit... But sometimes I think that I haven't actually quit, but am just resisting. Even now, it's sometimes really hard to resist that temptation."

I think of games as a way to pass the time or bond with your family while having some fun. But when I think about how my friends and many other people spend so much time playing games every day, it doesn't seem like a good use of time.

What I finally decided is that we ought to be careful about things that are too fun or enjoyable. Just as the most colorful mushrooms are poisonous and the most beautiful flowers can make you dizzy, I've come to think that too much fun must be some kind of trap. It's easy to confuse having fun and feeling good with being happy.

When something is too fun and enjoyable, the temptation to do it can sneak up on you when you're in the middle of some other activity, whether you want it to or not. That will make you miserable as well as distract you again and again from what you've been given to do each day.

With your mind in the grip of temptation, precious things sometimes slip away as if they were totally unimportant. If you're not careful, that temptation can become a habit and take control of your will.

"It's true that there's nothing wrong with games."

But it would make me sad to get distracted from my dreams and lose things of true value because of just one of the many things that can bring us happiness. If we let games become our focus and change the plans we have for our lives, I don't think the momentary pleasure they bring can be called happiness.

When it comes to achieving true happiness in our lives, the things we suffer, endure, and overcome can all be their own kinds of happiness. I think that what's truly important is not momentary pleasure but overall happiness, and I resolve to spend more time with the people who matter to me.

I think that what's truly important is not momentary pleasure but overall happiness, and I resolve to spend more time with the people who matter to me.

My mom

Let me tell you about my Mom! She always smiles at us. She's a grown-up, but she's no different from us. She'll run around with us and go up to the rooftop for a sword fight and climb on top of the car. She'll make a mess with us and tell stories and use her imagination, too. Mom is our friend - she takes naps, cries when she's sad and laughs when she's happy. She's even more of a prankster than we are, and sometimes her imagination is even better than ours. She can always get us to laugh by making up new stories on the spot. She's like an imagination box that's always up for telling another story when we ask for it. Whenever possible, Mom tries to do the things we want.

Mom can sometimes be stern, but we know that's not how she really feels. When she makes a point of being stern with us, we can't help paying attention, because we know what's in her heart. And when that happens, she later comes over to apologize.

We tell Mom we're sorry, too. Her saying sorry first makes us feel really bad for her. We sometimes get in fights, but we hug each other afterward.

When I have trouble doing sometimes, Mom waits until I can do it on my own. When I'm going through something difficult, she cheers me on and urges me to stay strong. I think those troubles and difficulties have helped me keep growing. When I used to ask Mom for help when I was having trouble making something, she would say, "Figure it out yourself. I could show you how this time, but when you run into something like this later, you'll have to deal with it on your own because Dad and I might not be with you then. You need to be strong enough to handle this kind of thing." I didn't use to understand what she was saying and got hurt when she told me that. But time has passed since then, and now I'm grateful that Mom and Dad didn't help me. When I'm making things, I don't ask questions anymore.

When I'm drawing plans, I ask Mom what she thinks, and I've gradually started coming up with new ideas. When my siblings and I get in a fight occasionally, Mom helps us make up. I think Mom is the wisest person I've ever met. She always encourages us to have a peaceful relationship, and she always helps us to move forward bravely. Mom says she wants me to be happy.

I'm not sure what I'll do in the future, but I want to do something that will make me happy and make other people happy as well. Mom is the connection between my siblings and me; she makes it possible for us to love each other before she tells us to. While I may move away from Mom when I grow up, I'll feel as if her actions, her words, and her image are still there inside me. I'll always remember Mom. She was the one who taught me what it means to live, love, and care for others. And thanks to Mom, I'll someday be able to teach my own children how I grew up.

The person known as Mom gave life to the person known as me. She was the one who brought my light into the world and helped me share that light with others. Tiny acorns like us are planted deep in the ground so we can grow into big oaks. Mom is my continuing source of strength both yesterday, today, and tomorrow. Mom, I love you, so deeply... Thank you for raising me and my siblings.

During the Fight

Date: April 2, 2019

Today, Mom got distracted while she was cooking something on the stove. The pot caught on fire, filling the house with a burnt smell. We couldn't sleep because of the smell, so the whole family went to the sauna, where people can stay for the night.

There was a playroom at the sauna, and my siblings and I went there to play. We'd been there for a while when we suddenly heard raised voices and then swearing. I was so surprised that I stopped playing and peered around like a meerkat. A man and women had gotten into an argument. In the playroom, the noisy voices of my siblings and friends were now replaced with the even louder shouting of grown-ups.

Soon after the two grown-ups started fighting, everyone in the sauna gathered to the playroom, and I realized the fight had become a spectacle.

"Where is it? Where is it?"

"Make some room! I want to see, too."

It felt strange to see all those goggle-eyed people craning their necks and standing on their tiptoes to get a better view of the fight.

With my siblings and even crawling little babies staring wide-eyed at the grown-ups, hearing all those curse words made me uncomfortable. I wanted to get my siblings out of there, but there were too many people crowded around us.

It made me truly sad that the pair of grown-ups were trying to shout over each other in a playroom full of kids and that everyone else was too busy watching to even try to break up the fight. The fighting went on for some time, and I lost myself in my own thoughts.

I sometimes quarrel with Wootae and Yudam and say mean things in hopes of winning an argument. But even if I win, before long I feel uneasy.

Hurting my siblings by shouting louder and saying nastier things isn't winning. I eventually get so uncomfortable that I apologize to them and realize how small I feel.

The man and woman were yelling hurtful words at each other. They were flinging around all the anger in their hearts, making the fight even worse without any thought for the people around them.

It's okay to have different opinions. But when people fight over those differences, there will be emotional damage.

The man and woman at the sauna must have felt extremely uncomfortable during their fight. I felt a little afraid that if we were to view their discomfort as nothing more than something fun to watch, we would have turned into people who just sit by and watch all the hurtful things happening around us.

A flower floats up

Date: April 14, 2019

The surging waves swallowed everything.

The pain of family members waiting for their children to come back,

the sadness of everyone who was watching and praying,

and even the truth itself sank into the ocean.

But amid all that awful pain,

a flower floats up,

a new love in bloom.

It's already been five years since we moved to Jeju.

I still clearly remember how the sinking of the Sewol ferry happened right after we arrived in Jeju, ripping so many people away from their loved ones. I remember days gloomier than any that had come before as so many people's sadness, anger, and frustration fell like rain.

We folded our hands and raised a fervent prayer, clinging to a slender ray of hope.

We beat our breasts over and over, we howled and wailed without finding the slightest relief... We kept up our ear-splitting appeals until deep into the night, without feeling afraid about how dark it had grown.

In the end, we had to accept they were gone with silent hearts. Even now, that anguished separation makes me sob and choke back tears.

I wish people wouldn't turn away from others' pain as if it had nothing to do with them.

Today, I lift up a quiet prayer in remembrance of that day. May that beautiful love never be wounded... May that beautiful love bloom and bring some measure of healing...

At Basilique de Montmartre

About the Feeling of Anger

Date: April 19, 2019

I was thinking about a story from the life of the Buddha that I heard in a debate class yesterday. When the Buddha stopped by a banquet to ask for something to eat, he was showered with curses. As he quietly turned around and left the building, one of his disciples got angry.

"Doesn't it make you mad to be cursed at like that?" the disciple asked.

We're told that the Buddha said, "I didn't accept the curses, so that person had to accept them instead. That's probably why he was angry."

The Buddha is really amazing!

When I get in a fight with my brothers, when I hear something that rubs me the wrong way (not even a curse!), or when someone offers an opinion that's different from mine, anger slowly rises up in me.

I'm often unable to keep my emotions from showing.

There are currents of anger hidden in the depths of my heart. But because joy is always in front of me, the anger is sometimes quick to disappear.

My anger is like sand tossed up from the sea each day. It's swept away only to be washed ashore again. I've pledged to not make a scene when my emotions rage. The wild waves could swallow not only me but other things as well, and ultimately bring unhappiness.

My emotions heat up when the hot sun shines down, and cool off when evening comes. Sometimes there's sadness in the rain, and when the snow of pain falls, it freezes my aching heart.

I feel countless emotions throughout the day, but anger is the toughest of them all. That's why it must be handled with particular care. I know I'll never be like the Buddha, but today I plan to start practicing how to better recognize the feeling of anger when it comes.

"I didn't accept the curses, so that person had to accept them instead. That's probably why he was angry."

There's nothing in the world that's exactly the same

Date: May 9, 2019

There's nothing in the world that's exactly the same. That's why I think we're all special. But we don't know we're special, and some people try to copy others by wearing clothes that don't suit them. They try to be like others and own things that others find pretty. They start following trends.

My younger brother Wootae's outfits are pretty random. At first, his bizarre and unique outfits seem both totally unplanned and carefully coordinated. He'll braid his hair in two ponytails and throw on a polka dot cardigan that my mother got as a present. He'll put on some tight black swimming pants with red or white socks and then yank the socks up to his knees. Then after all that, he'll run around in soccer shoes.

Today, Wootae wore his pants inside out when he came to pick up Yudam from school.

He was strutting along in front of school, with his arms swinging, when some woman came up and spoke to him. I watched them talk and then went up to Wootae.

"Who was that, Wootae? Someone you know?"

"No, I don't know her."

"So what did she say?"

"Well, she told me my pants were inside about and I should turn them right side out."

"So what did you say to that?"

"I told her I know, but that I'm not going to do that. This is comfortable to me, and I don't like being the same as other people!"

Wootae took it in stride and didn't make a big deal about it. And then this is what he said.

"Isoo, I'm the one and only in the world, right?"

At the front of the Rabu inn

Date: June 6, 2019

My school trip is turning out to be a fascinating, mysterious adventure.

It's amazing to think I'll get a glimpse into the life of Van Gogh, something I've been so curious about.

I could picture that great artist persevering through times of loneliness and hardship. Until this exhilarating moment, I knew next to nothing about Van Gogh. But we're connected by painting, without the need for anything else.

I love his faith.

I love his painting.

고흐가 머물렀더던 라부여관 앞에서. 1500.

Yudam's Sobs

My little sister Yudam started elementary school this
year, and she's been going for four months now. When
she first started, she was excited about being around
so many other kids and about the big sports field. She
headed to school with a light heart and a spring in her
step. I'd told Yudam to share lots of stories about school
with me, since I'm not attending school right now.

"Yudam, did you have fun today?"

"Yeah! Today we had dance and, um... we drew pictures
and learned hangul (the Korean alphabet), too."

"Wow! You're going to learn hangul even faster than I
did. I barely finished learning it before I turned eight."

"Yeah! I'm really good."

Yudam was talkative and cheerful when she came back
from school, full of energy and laughter.

But after a while, Yudam started getting irritable and bad-tempered.

"Yudam, did you have fun today?" I asked.
"Yeah."

Yudam started giving me one-word answers and stopped telling me stories about school. As a result, I guess I lost interest in what she had to say without even realizing it. Seeing Yudam getting irritated and angry with Mom so often made me worry that Mom was having a hard time. But when I told Yudam she should hold her temper, she just cried even louder and yelled at me for scolding her. After this went on for a while, Mom, Wootae, and I ended up telling Yudam during a family meeting that we were having a hard time because of her bad temper. Yudam said she understood and promised to deal with it, but she didn't actually change.

Our other siblings and I grumbled that she hadn't changed, and Mom eventually heard about it.

Mom held Yudam in her arms as she cried. "Mom! Why do I have this mole on my face? None of the other kids have one."

Somewhat cluelessly, Wootae piped up. "I have a mole on my hand, too, and it's huge! Isn't that cool, Yudam?"

Since Yudam was born, she's had a big mole, about the size of a fingernail, between her eyebrows. I heard that it used to be as faint as a smudge of dirt and that the doctor said it would fade and disappear over time. But instead, Yudam's mole gradually got bigger and darker.

Before going to school, Yudam had never complained about the mole. That's why we were all shocked when she suddenly made such a fuss about it.

We'd always loved how vivacious Yudam was. What made this an even bigger surprise was how Yudam had responded before when Mom said she'd have to get the mole removed eventually.

Yudam said she didn't want the mole removed because it was part of her and she loved it.

I couldn't stop thinking of how hard it would be for Mom to hold and comfort Yudam if she kept crying every day.

Mom said we shouldn't bother Yudam and should give her a chance to open up. But since we had to deal with her bad temper every day, a little seed of hate began to bloom in our hearts. We didn't understand why the mole was such a big deal, or why she'd suddenly started crying about it.

One day, one of our younger cousins came over. We filled a big tub with water and soon were busy playing in the water. When Yudam got home from school, she wanted to join us in the tub. But just then, our cousin abruptly said, "In that case, I'm going to go."

At that, Yudam grimaced and her eyes brimmed over with sad tears that soon poured down with a sound like thunder.

As we stared at Yudam, she told us an awful story that made time seem to stop. Listening to her, my heart began to ache.

"You guys don't get it!" she wailed. "You don't know how it feels. Every day, the other kids tease me because of my mole. When I'm in line at the cafeteria, they point at my mole. They shove and hit me, and when I ask them why, they say they're just goofing around. When I was playing dodgeball today, the older girls threw the ball at me, trying to hit my mole. Nobody likes me, and it's because of my mole. The older boys don't like me, either."

I had only wanted Yudam to get over her temper, but I hadn't been able to understand how she was feeling. I realized that I hadn't been thinking about it properly. She had a reason for everything she was doing, and I hadn't known that she was hurting so much. I felt so bad I called Mom over to talk with us, which was when Yudam began to sob.

I felt bad for Yudam. It made me think about how a little difference could make someone a target for teasing and discrimination from the other children. I let Yudam play in the water with me all day long, with the hope she would quickly recover from her heartache.

There's nothing wrong with being different from other people. I thought it was really strange that Yudam would be judged because of her mole.

That evening, I lay down to go to sleep, but sleep wouldn't come. As Yudam lay there with her back to me, she looked very small, and her old glee seemed to be gone.

It made me sad to think that the little girl who had thought of herself as being so pretty was now convinced she was so ugly. It seemed like her thoughts and feelings had been changed by what others had said.

I wish my younger sister Yudam had been able to brush off those words as if they were no big deal, but I guess I couldn't even have done that myself.

How could anyone say that to her, and how could I comfort her?

After a while, once Yudam had fallen asleep, I heard Mom sniffling sadly as she caressed my sister, cradling her in her arms. Today was a painful day for everyone in my family.

It seemed like someone's thoughts and feelings had been changed by what others had said.

The Old Woman at the Five-Day Market

Date: July 12, 2019

On Jeju Island, there are special markets held every five days. Whenever Mom says we're going to one of these five-day markets, I get excited. We have such a great time when we go—we get to eat snacks like bungeoppang (fish-shaped pastries) and hotteok (pancakes with a sweet filling), drink sikhye (sweet rice punch), and look around the market. The fun starts before we even arrive.

On one visit to a five-day market, Wootae got in trouble for gawking and putting his hands on everything. Then there was a loud "pop" right next to us that made us all jump backward. But it was just the rice popping machine, and we bought some of the freshly popped rice.

As we were moving through the market, I was shocked to hear someone shouting behind us.

Turning around, I saw an old woman selling something out of a basket in front of a shop, and the lady who ran the shop yelling at her to go away.

The old woman asked the shopkeeper to let it slide, but the shopkeeper cut her off and coldly said no.

The whole thing made me very uncomfortable. When I heard the shouting, I tugged on Mom's clothes and pointed toward the old woman, who was holding a black plastic bag and had just put a couple of abalone into the basket.

Mom said she didn't know why the shopkeeper was running the old woman off like that, either. As we walked by, Mom said to the shopkeeper, "Why is it that people aren't allowed to sell stuff on the street here?"

"There's a place for those old women to sell their wares, but instead of carrying on their trade there, they keep coming over here and getting in the way of other people's business!"

"You know, you could have spoken to her more politely. The whole thing struck me as unpleasant."

But the shopkeeper only replied, "You can't go easy on that kind of woman. If you're polite with them, they'll take it as an excuse to keep coming around!"

I felt upset. Taking my hand, Mom said there wasn't anything to be done. But as we made another circuit of the market, we ran into the old woman again. Squatting down in front of a telephone pole, she looked up piteously at Mom. "Abalone for sale! I've got plenty!"

Mom went up to the old woman and crouched down beside her. "How much are they?"

The old woman laid out 10 or so abalone in the little basket and said they cost 20,000 won.

"You know what, I'll take them! Is that all you were meaning to sell today?"

The old woman said she had the same number of abalone in the black plastic bag beside her.

"I bet all that squatting is hard on your legs. I'll take the rest of the abalone, too. Put them all in the basket."

"Goodness, you don't know how much this means to me… Thank you, thank you…"

The old woman thanked Mom again and again as she put the abalone into the basket, her hands trembling, tears in her eyes.

I felt grateful to Mom. If she had just passed by without buying the abalone, it would have weighed on my heart for the rest of the day. It was a relief to see the old woman heading back home after selling all her abalone.

Holding Mom's hand, I spoke to her in a whisper.

"Thanks, Mom. I don't usually like seafood, but I think I'll be able to eat this. And if you hadn't bought this, it would have really weighed me down."

Mom whispered in my ear, "Isoo, I used to squat down selling things in the marketplace just like her. It's hard to describe how desperately I wanted the people walking past to buy something from me. I couldn't just walk on because I've been there, and I know what it feels like. And plus, that old woman looked really sick, and it pained me to think of how hard her life must be.

The fact is, I don't know how to cook abalone. Let's give this to your aunt and ask her to fix something for us."

I just love how honest Mom is!

"You don't know how to cook abalone? All you have to do is toss it into some doenjang jjigae(soybean paste stew)!"

"Huh, you're right! I never knew it could be so easy. I guess I was thinking about something a little more gourmet."

"Hey, doenjang jjigae is gourmet."

We shared a big laugh as we happily went on our way.

Looking at the old woman walking away, I said the following prayer in my heart.

I hope the old woman we met today will be happy.

A little myself

That nasty customer called "anger" paid another visit today. The feeling of anger wriggled around inside before bursting out into the open. I've told myself I know how to deal with anger... Even so, it got the better of me once again.

Just like a phoenix, anger always seems to rise from the ashes. Even when I'm calm, anger can rise up inside, and its great power overwhelms me and wipes away other feelings—feelings that are joyful, shiny, and clear—in the blink of an eye.

It felt like I was dreaming, but the dream also seemed like a nightmare. Actually, the dream became reality.

I suddenly felt a terrible pain in my belly. Tears flooded my eyes, and an awful scream was forced from my mouth. Yujeong had leapt down from the wardrobe right onto my belly as I lay there sleeping...

A mighty anger swallowed me up.

The brilliant, wonderful feelings I'd felt everyday were plunged into darkness; the shining flowers that had always taught me about beauty bowed their heads and shriveled up. The colorful animals that had frolicked through my head had vanished without a trace, and I seemed to be encased in a shell made solely of sadness and anger.

Holding my belly, I slowly sat up. There in front of me was poor little Yujeong, her tiny hands trembling.

I thought of the story of the "empty boat" from a book that Mom had read one time in class.

In the book, someone is rowing across a river when a boat bumps into them. If the other boat is empty, the rower won't get angry, no matter how bad their temper is. But if someone is in the other boat, the rower will first shout at the other person to get out of the way, then keep yelling if they don't seem to hear, and finally start cursing at them.

All of that happens because someone is in the boat. But they won't shout or get mad if the boat is empty. If only we could empty our boat as it crosses the river of the world…

If I could empty my own boat, too, I wouldn't get angry.

A family friend who had come over scolded poor Yujeong for getting into yet another scrape, and then she came over to me and gently caressed my shoulder. That's her own way of saying she's sorry.

This trivial thing that happened to me today turned into great anger inside me, holding up a mirror to let me see a little more of what's inside my heart.

Once anger comes, the other feelings that are joyful, shiny, and clear disappear in the blink of an eye.

I wonder when I'll be able to control my emotions…

The Real Me

Date: September 28, 2019

If you look closely at people, it's clear how everyone is trying to look good for others. Our makeup, hairdos, and fancy clothing are supposed to make us look prettier and trendier, but sometimes it just seems to make us look worse.

People may as well be hiding themselves. If we worked on our true selves, rather than our outward appearance, we would learn the outward appearance means nothing. Little kids know that. They never pay attention to what other people think of them.

It's in our true selves that we live and breathe. Those who know how to dress up their true selves are the ones who dress up their hearts. They're the ones who change others for the better with the truth, rather than a lie; they're the ones who can laugh truly, from the heart.

I'm still young, and my heart is still young, so I've got to keep working on myself.

It's said that fruit tastes better and sweeter after going through the storm and the tempest. In the same way, I'll probably have to go through more trials if my heart is to become beautiful. I'll try to bravely accept those trials and hang on until I reach the other side.

Once again, I pledge to become beautiful, to become the real me…

Words That Lift Our Spirits

Date: October 9, 2019

My little sister Yudam doesn't know how to read by herself. But she likes being read to, and whenever I'm nearby, she wants me to read her a book. She seems to crave books all the more because she can't read them for herself.

After I went through one book with her, she held out two more books for me. Just when I was starting to get tired, Wootae came over and took over for me. He can't read very fast yet and often struggles to sound out the words, but he said he was happy to read to Yudam.

So Wootae started reading to Yudam. After a couple of books, he said aloud that he was getting tired because Yudam hadn't thanked him for reading to her. But, he added, if she said thank you, he just might have enough energy to read one more book.

That made me think about the mysterious strength that the simple phrase "thank you" can give us.

I realized that when those words enter our ears, the doors of our heart spring open with a flash, and we gain the power to do anything for someone else. Those wonderful words might even be enough to nourish each other's hearts.

After listening to Wootae, Yudam immediately said thank you several times and clutched the next book to her heart as she waited for him to read it, her eyes sparkling. Wootae may have been tired of reading by then, but he said he'd gotten an energy boost and started the next book, fumbling with the words in a loud voice. The scene made me smile.

Making an effort on someone else's behalf may be tough, but I think it also makes us happy. That's how we come to feel affection for each other. That's how we show each other our love.

Saying Nice Things I Didn't Really Mean

Date: October 21, 2019

A man came up to me today and said, "I saw you on TV yesterday... You must really have some bad manners if you talk down to adults like that. I guess your parents just didn't raise you properly!"

That must have been really hard to hear for Mom, who was right there beside me. When I make a mistake, Mom is the one who gets slammed for it, and all those attacks are painful.

Apparently, a fundraising program that I shot with some TV personalities was broadcast yesterday, and the fact that Wootae and I weren't using polite speech in Korean seems to have caused a problem. With a sigh, Mom said she's had a lot on her mind since this morning.

I have some indistinct memories from when I was little. Every day at daycare, I had to watch the teacher hit the kids.

Though she ordered us around, yelled at us, and bullied us, I just assumed I had to obey her because she was above me.

I wasn't able to express the things I felt. For two months, I kept those feelings inside and couldn't even tell them to Mom. The teacher told us not to tell anyone, and I thought that was the only way I could survive.

I couldn't stop feeling anger and hatred for other people. That emotional problem went on for a very long time.

What I didn't realize was how much effort Mom put into helping me get better during that time. After reading Mom's book, it was painful to imagine how hard that must have been for her.

I'm fine now, but I bet it's still tough for Mom. Since that time, she hasn't forced me to use polite speech because she wants me to be free to express my feelings.

I'm thankful to Mom for waiting for me to make my peace with both informal and polite ways of speaking instead of forcing me to learn them.

I didn't like it when the teacher made me say nice things I didn't really mean. I want to say nice things I really mean.

At some point, I realized that everyone deserves to be respected. That respect isn't made by using the polite sentence ending; the walls of our heart have to come down first. When we're worried or afraid about what other people will think of us, or stressed out about what we're not supposed to do, those walls instantly shoot up even higher.

For the first time in a while, I was able to let down my walls and relax with You Hee-yeol, Noh Hong-chul, and Jang Do-yeon, drawing pictures, playing guitar, talking, and having a good time together.

Before long, we had become good friends and were able to have a conversation not through our words but through our feelings.

People said I have bad manners because I use informal speech when I answer questions, without adding the polite sentence ending like the kids that grown-ups say are well-mannered.

But I think having good manners means doing for others as I'd like them to do for me. It means being considerate of other people's feelings and not bothering them with my behavior. That's something I'm working on.

I don't want Mom's feelings to get hurt anymore because of me.

I want to say nice things I really mean.

Becoming Free

Sometimes, I want to chase my heart's desire. I want to act on my feelings. But at times, I have to stop for a moment. Because I'm still young, acting on my feelings sometimes makes people around me uncomfortable. That can happen at airports, restaurants, museums, and cafés. When I act like that, I might get bad looks from a lot of people.

The thing is that children still have a lot of pent-up curiosity. I'm a fountain of curiosity. There are still many things I want to learn about and look into. My hands are always reaching out for something, words pop out of my mouth before I even know it, and my legs want to climb up on the couch and start jumping around. But I need to stop for a moment because that can hurt other people or make them uncomfortable.

How wonderful it would be if people would try a little harder to understand children's feelings and show them some consideration!

That would make me grateful and help me grow up to be an adult who is thoughtful and understanding of everything. By then, I would have positive habits both of mind and body that would allow me to follow my heart without making other people uncomfortable, rather than just suppressing my behavior.

Growing up without stress is only possible when everyone is thoughtful and understanding. True freedom means not getting bad looks from anyone even when you act on your feelings. I will train good habits until they come naturally to me so I can find that freedom.

How Many Wounds Did It Carry?

Date: October 27, 2019

When a passing cat caught sight of me, its back arched and its hair stood on end. It could have just approached me calmly...

The cat stared at me, its eyes full of fear. It wouldn't even give me a chance to show I wasn't a threat. I wondered how many wounds it carried...

Would animals like that cat be so wary if they hadn't faced any threats since arriving in the world?

I really wish I could speak calmly to other people, and that everyone could approach each other calmly.

I've been hurt, too.

Looking at that cat over there, I'm reminded of various parts of myself.

In my mind's eye, I can see the teacher at my old nursery school who hit children every day. I can see the eyes of the teacher at my next nursery school who locked me out of the classroom because I didn't come in right after lunch.

I couldn't go back inside and had to stand around in the sun for two hours...

Then there was the time I spent the entire day out of class, sitting there in the bathroom daydreaming...

When I share a cup of tea with Mom and talk about everything that happened back then, I'm reminded of how much I was hurt.

Those things don't bother me anymore. But at the time, the world was a scary place, and those were scary things...

Even now I sometimes freak out over nothing. Perhaps that's because all that fear and pain is still down there in my subconscious.

I think I can overcome and transcend the pain that lies dormant in my subconscious if I make a repeated and conscious effort. That's because I'm no longer the same person I was back then.

어떤 상처가 있길래...

I Walk to Clear My Mind

I realized I get a headache on days I do a lot of thinking. I tried to put my thoughts on hold, but my thoughts were walking ahead of me. And so I kept walking. I realized that my body and my feelings were getting lighter. Thoughts must be extremely heavy.

I got up one morning and was going for a run with Toto when a lady passing by shouted at me to stop.

The lady told me I needed to put Toto on a leash from 6:30 to 9:00 am because that's when she takes her little chihuahua for a walk on that path. Then she added that I should do the same from 7:00 to 9:00 pm.

Without really thinking it over, I agreed to do as the lady said. But my heart grew heavy on the way home.

I'd meekly given in to that scary lady's demand without giving a thought to Toto.

I felt bad for Toto, who was looking up at me. "From now on, I'm supposed to put you on a leash in the mornings and evenings!"

Once I got home, I told Mom what had happened, still feeling upset about it. Mom said that if Toto was bothering somebody, we didn't really have a choice.

But Toto doesn't bother anybody. If anything, he's so happy to see people that he keeps wagging his tail. It hurt my feelings when people assumed he was a mean dog just because he had black fur.

But the fact is that not everybody knows what I know. I reminded myself that the fact that something bothers other people can be reason enough not to do it.

Toto and I stayed outside for a long time on our walk.

This was the monologue running through my head. "That lady was really out of line! She even gave me specific times when Toto is supposed to be on a leash. She could just try to get to know Toto. That's what I would have done."

But of course, everybody sees things differently. After I'd recognized and accepted that, my mind felt at ease.

Showing You Care

Date: November 27, 2019

I woke up in the middle of the night with a sore throat. It hurt so bad that Mom took me to the emergency room.

I wasn't given any special medicine, just a painkiller. The next day, I seemed to be feeling better, and by that afternoon, I was playing as if nothing was wrong.

But that evening, I started to feel hurt by my family. They'd stopped asking if I was okay, which made me feel like they only cared about me when I was sick.

Then something occurred to me. Mom had told us about a lot of her aches and pains over the years, but I'd never asked whether they were gone now or whether they were still with her. I wondered how sad and lonely she must have felt.

That's when I learned that when someone says they're hurting, asking them how they feel even when they look okay will warm their heart with the knowledge that you're there for them.

I guess I should run over to Mom and ask her about all the aches and pains she's ever told me about. I'm going to ask whether she's better now... and whether anything else is hurting...

What do you think about

Day in and day out, my family is always getting into some kind of trouble. I wonder why those minor accidents seem like such a big deal to me right now.

Today, my little sister Yujeong wanted to fry an egg by herself, so she poured some cooking oil into the frying pan, turned on the gas, and waited for the oil to boil.

She must have been confused as to why the oil wasn't boiling because she turned the stove up even higher as she waited. But oil is different from water—it doesn't start simmering when it gets to 100 degrees.

Yujeong didn't notice that the frying pan was smoking. Tired of waiting, she cracked an egg into the pan, which splashed some of the burning oil onto her face and arms. Then, the oil-slathered frying pan caught on fire, which soon spread to the nearby window's curtains.

When we heard Yujeong's sudden shrieks, we came running over. In shock, we drew some water and threw it onto the fire, but the fire wasn't easy to put out.

The fire didn't spread too far, but it was terrifying to see flames leaping up before my very eyes. Mom came over and beat the fire with a towel until it went out.

As we stood there looking at each other, our eyes wide with shock, Yujeong giggled, as if she had no idea what had just happened. I was peeved that she'd given us all such a scare and was now laughing about it... "Do you think this is funny?"

Mom told me to cut it out and said that Yujeong had probably been scared, too.

Just then Yujeong began to cry and scream that her face and arms were in pain. Because of the accident, Yujeong had to soak her arms and face in ice-cold water.

The accident helped me see things from Yujeong's point of view, from Mom's point of view, and from the whole family's point of view.

Our daily routine is livened up by all these little accidents. I think they teach us something about how life works and what it means.

We get worked up over mistakes great and small, as well as our own thoughts. But in reality, none of it's a big problem.

I found myself thinking that as worried as I may be, when I look back at this later, I'll probably be able to laugh it off and say it was no big deal.

Why those minor accidents seem like
such a big deal right now?

If Food Fell from Heaven

Date: December 11, 2019

If food were to fall from heaven, no one on earth would ever starve to death...

My family went out to eat today for the first time in a while. Afterwards, on our way out of the restaurant, I saw leftover food piled up on the tables. Do they just throw away all that food? That question weighed on my mind for the whole drive home.

We have a couple rules at our house. The first is brushing your teeth and going to bed at the right time. The second is eating all the food on your plate.

Mom says that letting food go to waste makes her feel bad. While I'd heard her say that before, it didn't really hit home until now. But seeing all that food going to waste today made me feel bad, too.

I felt really guilty about letting the guy at the parrot farm order me some jjajangmyeon (noodles in black bean sauce) and then not being able to finish it.

I felt sorry when I heard that people in Africa bake mud cookies because they don't have enough to eat.

I'm over here whining about the food I'm given and carelessly throwing food away... and people over there are munching on dirt because they don't have the food I let go to waste...

It's sad that a lot of people on earth don't have enough food to eat a balanced diet. From now on, I'll focus on feeling thankful for my food at mealtimes. Instead of turning up my nose at things that taste bad and stuffing my face with things that taste good, I ought to eat in moderation, whether my taste buds crave the food in front of me or not.

Too Much Talk Will Tie You

Date: December 18, 2019

I'm really bad at talking. My tongue is often unable to keep up with the thoughts in my head, which get all tangled up.

I also speak slowly. When someone asks me a question, all my usual thoughts sometimes seem to evaporate. When I stand there, unable to say a word, my eyes dart around, my face flushes, and my hands get clammy.

At times, talking makes me feel stupid. And some days, when I get really worked up, I'll say the first thing that comes to mind.

I'm more likely to put my foot in my mouth with people who come over to our house a lot because I'm so comfortable with them. It's really upsetting to realize that I've hurt someone with something I said. I truly hate myself when that happens, so I'll run off and hide up in the attic.

"Isoo! What's the matter?" Mom will have to ask me the question several times before I finally open up and share my feelings.

"Mom, I sometimes say things without thinking and then immediately regret what I've said. But the words are already out of my mouth. It makes me so upset."

After listening to me, Mom said, "Isoo, that happens to me a lot, too. I think the hard thing about talking is that once you've said something, you can't take it back. I've been alive for more than 40 years now, but not long ago I had a really hard time because of something I said. Sometimes I've even promised myself to never open my mouth again. You're not the only one who deals with this. I think that each time you learn this, you'll get a little better."

It was a little comforting to hear I wasn't the only one dealing with this. But the very next day, I got so excited that I put my foot in my mouth again. A friend of my parents who often came by told us he was about to leave for Australia. I was really grateful to him for everything he'd done for us around the house.

But then, yesterday, I shot off my mouth again while I was bouncing off the walls with excitement.

"It's okay since you'll be gone soon."

"I guess it's no big deal that I'm going away! That's all I'm worth, huh?" he said, pretending to break into sobs.

The thing is that I like that guy, and I don't know why I would have said something like that. I'm always getting shocked by what I say and wishing I hadn't said it.

I've learned that it's not easy for people to tell if I'm joking or being serious, and that I have trouble controlling what I say when my feelings get ahead of me.

I felt bad for my parents' friend. I realized that I need to think about other people a little before speaking. Talking too much can get you tongue-tied.

If I Could Only Live to the Age of 20

Date: December 27, 2019

Grandpa told me that a long time ago, it was common to die before the age of 60. So those who made it to 60 would have a birthday celebration that we call 'Hwan-gap'.

But now people are supposed to live to the age of 100 or even 120. When I think about it, I guess people a very long time ago probably held a celebration when people were much younger than 60—maybe 20. I suppose that 20 years, 60 years, and 100 years aren't all that different. When you're just a mayfly, morning, noon, and evening are as long as a lifetime.

Just as earth time is different from human time, the times of our lives are only different in how they feel; age itself doesn't seem very important. We should probably think about how happily we've lived in the time we've been given. While I've been alive for 11 years, I pay more attention to the time ahead of me than to how much time has already passed.

If I could only live until the age of 20, I would spend the nine years I had left loving people as much as I could. Anything is possible when you love somebody. Thanks to that magical feeling, in the end I'd be able to say I'd lived a happy life.

Grandma, who is over 70 years old, told me that time has gone by so fast for her. Things that happened 70 years ago feel like they happened just yesterday. No matter how old you are, everything before today is yesterday, and the important thing is to keep smiling right now!

Isoo, 12 years old

A World of Your Own

Date: January 1, 2020

There's just one world, but every person seems to be in a world of their own. We each look at the world from our own point of view. I think there's fighting and hatred and wars because everyone has their own point of view.

In our house, each of my siblings and I see the world differently. That's why we argue, lose our temper, and get sulky. I think that what happens in my small family is similar to what happens everywhere else. For that reason, I need to try to be a good person inside my family if I'm to get along with others when I grow up.

This is something Mom told me one time. "If we change ourselves instead of waiting for the world or other people to change, then our families, other people, our society, our country, and the world will change, too."

I guess I may have gotten in the habit of thinking that my way is the right way even though I still don't know much of anything.

That's why I lose my cool and why my face turns red. To become a better version of myself, I've decided I need to be the one to change—for my siblings and for my family.

If I Were in Her Shoes

When I woke up in the middle of the night, Mom was sitting next to me. I could tell she was hurriedly trying to clean something up. Soon, I fell back asleep.

A few days passed, and then a few more. Every so often I would wake up in the middle of the night and see Mom doing the same thing. After that, she told me she was having trouble sleeping.

A long time ago, Mom said that if she didn't take sleeping pills, she wouldn't be able to sleep and would get a headache the next day. She told us during a family meeting around that time that she didn't want to take the pills anymore, but she also didn't want to be exhausted from lack of sleep. We all agreed to help her, but at some point, we forgot all about it.

I've said before that Yujeong is mentally several years younger than her real age. She's behind in every area and can't understand a lot of words, but only our family knows about that.

When other people talk to Yujeong, she acts and answers as if she knows more than she does, so people don't see anything different about her.

I know all about this, but I often seem to forget it. Whenever Wootae, Yudam, and I get fed up with Yujeong, Mom gives us a hug and talks to us while trying to understand how we feel.

But before long, we get irritated again. We gripe about how Yujeong keeps getting in the way and doing things she's not supposed to do.

I don't know when that all started. I told myself I wouldn't act like that, but I haven't been able to keep my word. I hate Yujeong when she messes up my writing and drawing projects, and it's hard to avoid her when I'm writing or drawing, too.

One night, Mom was sitting there again when I woke up from my sleep. I'd been tossing in my sleep because of an icky feeling. As it turned out, my pajamas were wet.

Mom whispered in my ear, "Isoo, I'm sorry. Can you get up for a moment and stay quiet? I need to change your clothes. Yujeong wet the bed, and your pajamas got wet, too. Can you stay positive and not get upset for me?"

Mom wiped me down with a wet towel, dressed me, put down some clean sheets, and then put me back to bed. At that point, I was able to go back to sleep, but Mom still had to bathe Yujeong, dry her off, and do the laundry, too.

Mom has to work all day long, and even at night, she has to work instead of sleeping. The next day, I hated Yujeong for making trouble for Mom every night. "Mom," I said, "Yujeong keeps you from getting any sleep, and she gets in my way, too. That makes me mad!"

This is what Mom told me.

"Yujeong didn't choose to be born with that kind of disability. What if you and Yujeong were switched at birth? What if Yujeong has this disability instead of us?

Isoo, I would still be okay even if you wet the bed at night like that. I think Yujeong is here not to make things harder for you kids but to help you grow up and learn how to deal with anything that comes your way. If you get tired, come to me, and I'll give you a hug. We can work it out together."

After listening to Mom, I thought things over for a long time. I imagined that Yujeong had taken that disability on my behalf... Instead of being thankful that I was born the way I am, I have only felt irritation and resentment for how Yujeong gets in the way.

I made up my mind to rethink the situation with Yujeong and imagine being in her shoes. I also felt bad about not being able to do anything for Mom when she was so tired.

When will I be able to grow up? When will I become more mature in my thoughts and actions?

The stars in the night sky are shining even brighter tonight. It's as if they're comforting me. Or maybe they're the ones who want to be comforted.

Something Exciting

After breakfast, I hurried to brush my teeth and then hopped onto my bicycle. I didn't hear Mom tell me to put my scarf on. I didn't feel cold.

My siblings all followed me outside, including Yudam, who had recently learned to ride a bike.

As I was riding around the sports field, Yujeong said, "Isoo, where is the electricity?"

"What do you mean?"

"Where is the electricity?"

I didn't know what to say because I didn't understand the question. But then Yujeong pointed to her eyes and said, "Mine is here."

Without really thinking about it, I pointed to my chest as I made another loop around the field.

Yujeong shouted, "Say it one more time!"

I told her no and rode off in another direction.

But then I started feeling funny.

Why would Yujeong ask something like that? Did she think that people run on electricity, too?

My feet pumped the pedals and brought me back around to Yujeong.

"Yujeong, why did you ask that question?"

"What?"

"You know, you asked where the electricity is."

"People will die if they don't have electricity. You have to recharge too if you want to keep going."

"So how does Wootae recharge?"

"When he's dancing."

"What about Mom?"

"For Mom, it's exercise. She gets sick if she doesn't exercise.

"So how do I recharge?"

"When you're eating.

"And Dad?"

"When he plays with us."

"So what about you?"

"When I watch a movie!"

Considering that watching movies is Yujeong's favorite thing to do, she seemed to be saying that we're recharged by what we find exciting.

Actually, eating isn't the most exciting thing for me, but it must have looked that way to Yujeong.

After going home, I sat down and thought about where my electricity might be. Maybe I get recharged from my hands. I can use my hands to hug people. That's what seems to give me strength.

I hope the things my hands can do will give me even more strength later. I hope that Yujeong's electricity will turn out to be something exciting for me, too.

"Where is your electricity?"

My heart feels heavy

Date: March 7, 2020

The road that used to be scary because of the fast cars is now empty, and I didn't even notice when it happened.

Even when I ride my bike as fast as I can, it feels lonely because there's no one around.

Outside the window, only dried leaves are blowing around, as if they don't know anything.

The coronavirus has kept many people stuck at home.

It feels like it's been a long time living with this fear.

Today, while driving back home with my mom after grocery shopping, I was staring out the window when I saw an old man struggling to push a cart full of scrap paper.

On an uphill road, he was carrying that heavy, mountain-like load with his small body, facing away from the sun, and pushing the cart with heavy steps.

His arms were shaking as they pushed the huge load that looked like it could spill out at any moment, relying on his feet to keep going.

In the long shadow he cast, there was a deep sorrow hidden, a sorrow I couldn't fully understand.

I can't stop thinking about that old man.

Even in these times when everyone is living in fear, he's quietly doing what he needs to do.

It's a job he has to do every single day, whether he likes it or not, no matter how hard it is, because it's necessary to survive.

My heart feels heavy.

I have a lot on my mind.

To Mom 2

Mom!

I called to you because I'm thinking of you again right now, just as I've done so many times today. Never in my life have I forgotten you, not even for an instant. I always carry you around in my heart so we can spend time together.

When I'm busy with something else, I'll make a point of thinking about you, which warms my heart. When you leave us behind to go on a trip, my heart burns with missing you. When you're away, you occupy all my thoughts, and I silently call to you.

I realized something then: It's easy becoming a mother, but it's not easy being the kind of mother whose child will always smile to think of you. I can think of you a thousand times a day without getting tired of you. You always make me smile.

I really like you. I like you more than I can say.

I always want to think of you, to respect your thoughts,

and to share your heart. I hope we can be happy again

today. Mom, I love you. Thank you.

To Mom 3

Date: March 21, 2020

When I make a mistake while walking by, I often get scolded, so even though I want to do better next time, fear comes first.

Because of that, the world seems a bit scary to me.

I think it's because I'm still young.

But the reason I can still enjoy myself and run around freely, full of curiosity, is that my mom is always watching over me.

Just knowing that helps me see the world in a warmer light.

Today, I want to write a letter to my mom.

Then she'll write back, and I really enjoy waiting for her reply.

In that way, we share our hearts like petals coming together to form a flower, and we become flowers too.

I want our home to be full of those flowers.

Mom!

A long ago, you told me that when my body and mind are full-grown, I'll someday leave your nest and fly into my future, into a world that's brimming with hope. You said I'll be free to fly where I want to go, while doing the things I want to do… But sometimes remembering what you said makes me afraid. The world I've seen over your and Dad's shoulders isn't always a nice place. That's why I feel more scared.

What if I fly straight into the ground? You wouldn't be there beside me. Right now, the world is still so scary. Will I be able to do a good job? Someday, I'll be able to calmly fly into another world as I feel the wind between my wings.

But the thought that you won't be there makes me insecure. At the same time, I want to visit amazing and wonderful places around the world and see and experience many new things.

Mom, just like you said before, good people have good people to look after them.

I want to be a good person when I grow up, too, just like you. And I want to meet good people and help others smile. Having good people in my life and good things happening should give me a lot of courage, right? The courage that I get then will be thanks to you.

Mom, you've always been a rock to me!

When I think of you while I'm flying around the world, I want to always come back to you and tell you so many things. And then I want you to tell me many things, just as you do now. Thank you, Mom. I love you. You always give me strength.

A Present for Children's Day

Date: May 5, 2020

I sat on a boulder to take a little break. Catching my breath, I gulped down some water and wiped away my sweat.

The cool breeze felt good on my skin. After wetting my throat and catching my breath, I could see in front of me again. As I stared at the leaves dancing in their natural simplicity, I could feel the immense beauty of the sunlight shimmering on them.

It made me think that the world's greatest works of art are hidden around us in nature. If we look carefully, we can find colors and shades more remarkable than anything we've ever known. Maybe what Vincent van Gogh strove and struggled to express were colors most of us never get to see.

On a big bicycle outing with Mom and my siblings, I was panting as I biked what felt like a very long uphill stretch. Water shimmered desperately before my eyes.

I realized that it was the most delicious water in the world.

As we kept going on and on, and without any restaurants coming into view, my little brother Wootae got so ravenously hungry that dinner that evening became his present for Children's Day.

Naturally, I was thankful for everything today and felt sorry for taking such blessings for granted.

Half of the World Is Starving

I've learned from photographs, videos, and books that my friends on the other side of the world have different lives from me. I don't know what it would feel like to go there myself. Truth be told, I might get so upset I'd just burst into tears.

People over there are struggling for the lack of food and clothing, and some of them even die from sickness. But here I am, lacking for nothing, eating my fill. I feel guilty. I just feel guilty.

I would like to reach out a helping hand to my friends far away with the pictures I draw and the other things I can do. I think that everything ought to be used in common, so I want to be the first to share many of the things they need over there. Because we're all in this together.

We apparently grow enough food to feed everyone on earth. But some people are so overfed that they throw food away, while others are so underfed that they drink muddy water and eat mud cakes as they waste away. I think we should quickly find a solution for these issues, which aren't due to a food shortage but to food not being evenly distributed. I don't want anyone else to starve to death.

I drew this picture while thinking about the ragged breath of my dying friends.

My feelings go out to the profound sorrow of their breathing.

It brings tears to my eyes, and tears to my heart.

Those Who Are Dear to Me

All four of us siblings have our own tasks.

At every family meeting, we decide what we can do on our own and diligently apply ourselves to the task. Yudam, who wants to become a chef, boldly said she could handle making breakfast, and so that task was given to her.

When I got up this morning, just like any other day, Wootae and I took turns reading the Chinese characters we've learned and then listened to Mom read a book to us for our morning routine.

I felt especially hungry this morning, probably because I didn't eat much last night. But Yudam's breakfast preparations dragged on and on, and I kept waiting and waiting. Even while I was reading the Chinese characters, I kept peeking at her, wondering when she would call us over to eat. We were supposed to have toast for breakfast, and I felt that even if I stuffed a whole slice in my mouth, it wouldn't be enough.

Just when Mom had read the last page, a plate with a piece of toast finally appeared in front of me. My happiness was interrupted by an involuntary shriek.

"Yuck! What is this?"

The crust was burned black, and the toast was completely drenched in ketchup.

Yudam bent her head in discouragement, and then she snapped at me.

"Don't eat it, then! And after all that effort."

I responded with even more irritation. "Do you know how long I was waiting? How am I supposed to eat this? It's all burnt up!"

"Then you try making breakfast!"

With an expression of surprise, I raised my voice at Yudam. "Why are you getting mad?"

Wootae, who was sitting next to me, just stared bleakly at the blackened toast with tears in his eyes. He's had a tremendous appetite recently; he eats even more than me.

Yujeong was cluelessly parroting what I'd said. I suddenly felt very sad, and very hungry, too.

Mom had been quietly watching the scene. Then she called me and Wootae over and told us a story.

"A long time ago, when I was helping out in the kitchen at home, I got tired of being sent on errands when I really wanted to cook. So one day while your grandmother was out, I decided to cook a pork cutlet. I placed the cutlet in the frying pan and poured oil over it, and the curtains ended up catching on fire. I'd expected your grandmother to lose her temper and chew me out, but she just said, 'Even so, that tastes pretty good.' You have no idea how grateful I felt.

"Yudam wanted to show off her first culinary accomplishment, but since nobody likes her food, she probably doesn't want to cook anymore. I bet she isn't a big fan of you guys anymore, either. Burnt toast is something that can be fixed in no time, but Yudam's burnt feelings aren't so easy to fix."

After hearing Mom's story, I felt bad for Yudam. I hadn't given her credit for the effort she'd put into making breakfast, and I was worried that I'd made her lose interest in her dream.

So I went over to Yudam and cautiously raised the subject. "Yudam, I'm sorry for saying that after you worked so hard to make breakfast."

But she just said, "I don't like you," and stormed into her room, which was discouraging. Mom suggested that I give her a little more time.

We all sat around the table, keeping company with our own thoughts as if we'd planned it that way. After 10 minutes or so, Yudam quietly walked up to me and said, "I'm sorry, Isoo. I didn't mean to burn the toast, but it all happened so fast. I won't burn the toast anymore." And then she started to cry.

I quietly gave Yudam a big hug.

We sometimes take out our anger and irritation on the people we're closest to because we feel comfortable around them. Afterward, we insist that's not because we don't care about them or don't love them. But I've learned that if I'm careless with the people I'm close to because I feel comfortable around them, treating them carelessly will eventually change my feelings for them, regardless of how I originally felt.

And so, I've made up my mind once again to form positive habits.

I think that being nicer and kinder to the people I am close to will make my heart kinder and our relationships better, too. I also think that if more and more people's relationships improve in that way, society as a whole will become brighter and more beautiful.

This is what I want to say to the people who are dear to me:

Thank you. I love you.

Being nicer and kinder to the people
I am close to will make my heart kinder
and our relationships better, too.

Yudam's Lies

I'm not exactly sure how it all started.

I was hard at work on my chores to save up money for the school trip planned for October. I figured I would need to buy souvenirs and treats on the trip, and I was also sure that going somewhere new would give me stuff to write about.

I cleaned the house in the morning, weeded the yard, and washed the car on the weekends, and my piggy bank gradually began to fill up.

One day, I was shopping at the market with Mom and my younger siblings when we stopped in front of a restaurant selling tteokbokki. Just as I began to salivate at the thought of the delicious rice cakes in their sweet-and-spicy red sauce, I heard something that perked up my ears.

"Isoo, I'll buy some for you! Let's eat!"

"Wow, are you serious?"

"Yeah!"

I felt so thankful to Yudam, who seemed delighted at the chance to buy something tasty for us.

"Hey, Yudam, I didn't know you had any money!"

"Yeah, Grandma gave me some pocket money. Didn't you know?"

"I didn't! Okay, I'll take you up on that offer. Can I have some odeng (fish cake), too?"

"You bet!"

Wootae and I scarfed down our food, and Yudam paid the bill. She was really enjoying herself. Her face was beaming with a joy brighter than anything I'd seen until that moment.

When I rode my bicycle to school to pick Yudam up the next day, we stopped by a convenience store because I was feeling thirsty. But once again, Yudam pulled some money out of her pocket before I could.

"Let me get this for you, Isoo," she said.

When the family went out to a restaurant as a treat, Yudam said, "Mom, I'm going to cover the tab."

Mom said, "Yudam, where are you getting that kind of money from?"

"Well, I got some pocket money from Grandma, you know. I mean, it was a little while ago. A little while…"Is that so? And you're planning to cover the bill with your pocket money? Is that the best way to spend it? You could save it up until there's something you need or want to do!"

Yudam responded right away.

"Mom, I like buying food for the family even more."

We all stared at Yudam, feeling grateful, but also a little sorry. It made me think long and hard about how I'd been planning to use all the money I'd saved up to buy stuff for myself on my trip.

I made up my mind to surprise Yudam with a gift of her favorite snack. As soon as I got home, I opened up my piggy bank.

But what I found came as such a shock that I let out a screech.

Shocked by the sound, Wootae ran over and sized up the situation. "What happened, Isoo? It looks like a robber got into the house. Wait, what about my piggy bank...?"

Wootae scampered off and before long, I heard a scream from his direction.

I took another look inside my piggy bank, hoping I'd missed something, but it looked as if nearly a year's work had all vanished. The sadness in my heart turned into tears that ran down my face.

Wootae and I sighed and stared down at the ground. But then Wootae said, "If we can't do anything about it, we ought to just forget about it."

"You're right, but that's not easy, and it will take some time. By the way, how much had you saved up?"

"50,000 won for me."

"What? You saved up 50,000 won in a year?

I had 400,000 won!"

"Okay, but does it really matter how much money you had? We've got to get over it."

"Even though you had 50,000 won while I had 400,000 won?" That made Wootae pause for a moment.

"Isoo, I guess we'll need some time to get over this. Take some time and then let's go fly an airplane," Wootae said and then ran off.

Feeling sad, I went to Mom and told her the whole story. After I was done, she sympathized with me and said she could tell how upset I was. Then she told me several stories about losing things.

I told Mom that if she gave me some time I'd be able to get over it. Hearing her stories helped me calm down. Once I started thinking this wasn't a big deal, it turned out that it actually wasn't.

After a few days, Yudam came up to me and started quietly calling my name. But she wouldn't say anything else.

"What is it? What happened? Go ahead and tell me," I said.

At that, Yudam started to wail. "Isoo, the thing is... the thing is... that I... took ... your... money."

A lightbulb went on in my head. Come to think of it, she had kept offering to buy me things.

But when she pulled out those bills, I'd just assumed that she had saved up a lot of money. I'd never imagined she could have stolen mine.

Quietly, I wrapped my arms around her.

"Yudam, I'm very thankful that you could be so honest with me. If it were me, I don't think I could have done that. I'm not that brave, which makes you better than me. I was upset at first, but I've gotten over it now. Wootae got over it even faster than me! But why did you take the money?"

"I'm sorry, Isoo... I wanted to do something for the family. I can't do anything for you guys. But I didn't realize how much money it was."

Today, I got a glimpse into Yudam's heart. She had meant well—she'd wanted to act on her earnest desire to do something for other people—but she chose a pretty bad way of doing that.

She didn't know what she was doing, but I think she should have a chance to learn now. With my 400,000 won, Yudam got the joy of doing something nice for her family, and she also learned that she can't just steal things from other people. That feels like a better use for the money I'd saved up than whatever I would have bought with it.

I don't regret how my money was spent at all. This is one of those things my little sister Yudam has to learn as part of growing up.

Before going to bed, Mom gave me a hug and said, "Yudam asked me to wait until she could tell you herself. She said she didn't feel brave enough."

"Wait a second, Mom! So Yudam told you about this first?"

"Yeah."

"How did that happen?"

"I had told Yudam a story. Not long after that, she started crying up a storm and told me she had something to confess."

"What story was that?"

"I'll tell you that story later. Good night."

To Mom 4

When Mom is sick, I feel a bit heavy-hearted.

Every morning, she's always so busy, and even though I know that everything she does is for us, we just keep taking it all for granted.

When I ask, "Mom, aren't you tired?" she always says, "I'm not tired. I'm fine. Just seeing you all happy and joyful makes me really happy."

Then she adds, "Isu, thank you so much for asking."

She never forgets to say that.

To me, it sounds like she's also reminding me that it's important to pay attention to how others feel.

Mom seems to do more than other moms.

I know that Yoojung's situation adds a lot to her workload, and it must be really tough, but when I see her moving around all day without even sitting down, it makes me think that being a mom is a really hard job.

That must be why she's sick.

Mom!

When you're upset, I can't force myself to smile. The fact that you're upset makes me upset, too. When you're glad, I can feel my lips lifting into a smile. The fact that you're glad makes me glad, too.

Mom! You're like a pillar holding me up. When I'm having a hard time, you seem to say, "Hang in there! I'm here for you." Thanks to you, I've been able to stand tall. Thanks to you, I'm able to stand tall right now and will be able to do so again. But since you haven't been feeling well, I found myself wondering what would happen if you died. That was a terrifying thought, and it made me sad.

Mom! I hope you have a long and healthy life. I hope you'll stay here with me for a long time to hug me and teach me with your wise words as you do now. Is that too much to ask?

Mom, I hope you'll get well soon so that you can climb Mt. Halla with me. So once again today, I will say this prayer: "Please turn Mom's sickness into a flower."
Mom, thanks for staying strong for me again today. I love you.

"Please turn Mom's sickness into a flower."

Call me "Hyung"

Date: September, 2020

My aunt is someone who really cares about age. She even goes so far as to divide people based on their exact birthdates. It's hard for me to understand this way of thinking, and it's even harder to accept it. Today, Wootae is feeling pretty down and hasn't said much. He's been told that he has to call his cousin, who's the same age as him and who he hangs out with both at school and at home, "Hyung" (which means older brother in Korean). This is hard for Wootae to suddenly accept. Honestly, I don't really get it either. His cousin was born in August, and Wootae was born in November, so just because his cousin was born two and a half months earlier, he's supposed to be the older brother. Even at school, the teacher told Wootae that his cousin, who's in the same class, is technically his older brother. When Wootae asked, "But aren't we friends?" the answer he got was, "He's older because he was born first. Even with twins, the one who's born first is the older brother."

At school, the teacher gathered all the students and had them reveal their birthdates to sort them by age, from oldest to youngest, and then assigned titles like "hyung" and "dongsaeng" (younger sibling). How are we supposed to spend the next year studying together when we're divided like this?

Every time Wootae goes to school now, he hangs his head and doesn't say much. That one word—being told to call his cousin "hyung"—has made things awkward between them, even though they used to get along so well. Now, Wootae doesn't joke around or have fun like he used to; he's become quiet. I can't believe it. Just because adults decided who's older and who's younger, Wootae's mood, his thoughts, and even his days have changed. Is it really that important to divide people into "older" and "younger"?

I don't like it when people call me a "genius" or a "prodigy." I'm just "Isoo." I'm just one person among many. But people always want to put labels on things, dividing people into categories like genius and fool, older and younger, rich and poor, human and non-human, strong and weak, good and evil, adult and child.

I wish people wouldn't separate others based on what they see on the outside. I think it would be better if we could just respect and think of each person as an individual, as a life, like the people passing by outside the window.

When I judge someone, they'll judge me too. If I try to separate people, they'll try to separate me too. These kinds of divisions and prejudices make me uncomfortable. I believe that if we approach others with an open heart, without dividing or categorizing, and just accept things as they are, the world would be much warmer. And that warmth would come back to us as a love even greater than the one we gave.

What Do We Do About Yudam?

Date: October 15, 2020

Once a month, we clean out our closets. We started doing this because Yudam became obsessed with something. On the day we were moving, Mom was packing our stuff when something caught her by surprise. She lowered her head and heaved a sigh.

Tucked away in the corner of the closet, in a dark space behind the desk, were several black plastic bags caked in blue mold. When we smelled the stench rising from those bags and spotted blue particles of mold floating in the air, we all screamed.

"What on earth is that? What could have made such a strange smell?"

Yudam had filled the plastic bags with some clothes that Grandma or our aunt had bought her, along with some hoppang buns, boiled corn on the cob, three pieces of candy, and five hot dogs we'd bought at the five-day market.

Then she'd rolled the bags up and hidden them away where no one would look. She had apparently intended to eat the snacks by herself without us knowing.

The clothes she'd never worn were covered in mold. And since she'd gotten bigger in the meantime, she never would get to wear them, anyway.

Yudam lowered her head and then raised it again, with wide eyes and a guilty look.

"I was saving it so I could share it with everyone later. But why did the food go bad?"

Yudam didn't seem to realize that food can rot. I thought the whole thing was very interesting.

She started to cry while asking how the hot corn had gotten so moldy. Mom started talking to Yudam about a number of things. After listening to Mom, Yudam came over to us and said she was starting to feel sorry.

Through her sniffles, she told us she'd thought that if she shared with Yujeong, Wootae, and me, there wouldn't be anything left for herself. But now she realized how selfish she had been.

A few months later, Yudam had another surprise for Mom. She brought over some holey socks and told Mom she needed to buy some new ones. Mom said she'd thought it was strange that Yudam was always wearing holey socks and worn-out clothes.

"Don't you have some new clothes and socks? Why are you only wearing these holey socks, instead of the new ones?"

"I lost all my socks, and I shared some with Yujeong. I need some new ones!"

Since Mom had already been thinking Yudam might need some socks, she took her on a long-awaited trip to the store and bought her some socks she liked.

But that same day, Yudam got in a fight with Yujeong over a pair of socks, each claiming the socks belonged to her. After watching the fight, Mom poked around in the closet in Yudam's room and came upon a big plastic bag. Several dozen pairs of socks came tumbling out of the bag.

The bag was stuffed full of new socks that Mom had bought for Yudam and even more she'd gotten as gifts. Mom was dumbfounded and could only manage a heavy sigh.

I watched Mom sitting there wordlessly, her head drooping wearily. From behind, she looked so very sad.

Yudam had lied to Mom again. Yudam seemed very agitated about the family finding out about something only she was supposed to know. Her face contorted and she began to cry as if her world was collapsing.

Quietly, without saying a word, Mom embraced Yudam. Then she said, "Yudam, I love you so much."

Hearing that made Yudam's sobs all the louder. "Mom, I'm sorry," she said, almost wailing. "Mom, I'm sorry... I'm really sorry."

Even to my ears, Yudam sounded sincere. Mom kept talking, trying to figure out what had happened.

"Yudam, I'm sure you remember the promises you made.

I'm also sure the reason you broke those promises is because you thought your decision was more important than them. So I want to hear your side of things. Can you tell Mom why you didn't keep your promise? I trust you."Yudam wiped away the tears that kept flowing.

"Mom, I'm sorry... I'm sorry..."

Mom gave Yudam a hug and said she could have a little time. Mom seemed to be thinking about something, and Yudam sat quietly thinking, too.

After a couple of hours, Yudam went over to Mom and tugged on her clothes.

"Mom! I've made up my mind. I'm not going to disappoint you again. The thing is that I'm not even sure why I did that. Mom, I really hate Yujeong. It's just a feeling I have. I just hate how she treats me one way when you're there and another way when you're not. I don't know why she's like that. I hate how she's always hitting and pinching me and saying mean things to me.

I didn't want Yujeong to take my stuff, and I didn't want to share with her either. I guess that's why I kept hiding things and hoarding new stuff instead of using it."

When I thought about it, it did seem that Yujeong had behaved like that with Yudam more than with me or Wootae. Mom gave Yudam a big hug and listened to everything she had to say. Then Mom said she understood. She said she would watch Yudam and Yujeong more closely in the future. But she also said that Yudam needed to correct her behavior and asked her to lay down her craving for things once a month.

Mom said that Yudam needed to think about whether she really needed her possessions, how long she should keep them, and whether she could give up the things she treasured the most if someone else needed them more than her. So now, once a month, we put everything we need into a box we've been given and send everything else to people in need. Mom took me aside and said,

"Isoo, I'm really sad. After what happened today, how are we going to fill the empty place in Yudam's heart? I've got a lot to think about. Yudam's heart needs to be filled not with things but with our family's love and attention, and I get the feeling that we haven't been paying enough attention to her. We have to realize that hatred is a feeling that comes when you don't love yourself enough. We need to be more loving to Yudam. I don't think this happened because she's greedy. I think that she isn't the only one to blame here and that this is something we should all be thinking about."

I spent a lot of time thinking about what happened to Yudam today. I want to be more like Mom, who cares more about whether Yudam is getting enough love and attention than about the fact that she was greedy and didn't want to share.

A lot of things like this happen at our home. But I comfort myself with the thought that we'll turn out okay.

Hatred is a feeling that comes
when you don't love yourself enough.

This Much Is Enough!

In my family, we organize our closets once a month. I don't need a lot of clothing. Three T-shirts and three pairs of pants are enough.

I keep only the three shirts and three pairs of pants I wear the most and pass along everything else. I wash the clothes I've never worn and send them to kids at the orphanage, and I throw away the clothes that are ripped or stained with paint. I also hand down clothing to Wootae. What's really strange is that our amount of clothing stays the same even though we sort out our stuff once a month.

The clothes I give to Wootae usually have big holes or a lot of paint stains on them. When people see him, they often say he looks a little messy. Fortunately, Wootae isn't bothered by that.

Clothing isn't that important to us. The main thing is wearing something to protect your skin.

Wootae sometimes plays jokes with his clothing. He'll wear it inside out, soak it with water when it's hot outside, or cut off one pant leg.

One time, we went over to someone's house. It was a big and sprawling place. There were four people in the family, but they could only live in one of their five rooms. Of the other four, one was for storage, one was for clothes, one was for books, and one was for furniture.

In the end, rooms that were meant for people to live in were so packed with possessions that they weren't usable. If the family were to have to move, I doubt they would be able to go anywhere smaller because of all their stuff. Their possessions had taken over their house! That gave me a strange feeling.

Closet cleaning days put me in a good mood. It kind of feels like setting down a heavy bag you've been carrying around.

Mom told me once that she loves the feeling of stepping into a room that's completely empty, with nothing inside. I didn't understand what she meant at the time, but I sometimes think of that when I'm going through my things and deciding what to throw away.

Holding on to things we don't really need can be tiring. If I can content myself with a single trunk filled with the things I really need, I think my life will feel much lighter and much freer.

Wounded Feelings

Today was a very busy day. We had to go meet someone who was coming from the mainland at 1 p.m. I was in such a rush to finish my morning class that I still hadn't eaten lunch as the appointment drew near. Mom, Dad, Wootae, and I had to quickly decide whether to grab a bite to eat before the appointment, or whether to put off lunch until later.

But Wootae was so hungry that Mom suggested we eat at a sundubu (soft tofu) restaurant she knew in the area. She thought that if we called in our order and ate as soon as we got to the restaurant, we could still make our appointment. So she hurriedly called in the order, and we got ready to eat as soon as we arrived.

But when we got there, the waitress asked us what we wanted to eat. When Mom said we'd placed our order over the phone, the waitress said, "We didn't get any orders. Are you sure you didn't call a different restaurant?"

"Is there another branch of this sundubu chain?"

"Yeah, there's one other."

"Oh no," Mom said, with surprise and confusion on her face. "So where exactly did I call? What do we do?"

Dad suggested that Mom quickly call the other restaurant, which is what she did. She said she was sorry several times in a very apologetic voice. She honestly admitted her mistake and said she didn't know how to convey how sorry she was.

"I'm really, really sorry. I don't know how I made such a mistake," Mom said and then abruptly stopped talking. The three of us stared as she held her phone against her ear, breathing hard, hands trembling. Then all of a sudden, she began to cry.

Dad, Wootae, and I asked Mom what was wrong over and over, but she didn't reply. We kept staring at her. We held our spoons in midair and couldn't bring them to our mouths. It was painful to see Mom crying wordlessly.

What had happened? Some man had been talking loudly over the phone. What could he have said to make Mom shake like that?

Dad kept prodding Mom to explain what the man had said. "What did he say to you? Did he curse at you? What was it?"

Mom said that she was fine and that it wasn't a big deal.

But Dad said, "I'd better call him back. What on earth could he have said to make you cry?"

Mom told Dad not to call. She pointed out that people take things in different ways and that the man had every right to get mad at her mistake.

But my heart was still aching. Mom had made an honest mistake, and the man at the restaurant had apparently cussed her out. Mom said she wasn't willing to repeat what he'd said.

The curse words the unseen man had spoken so casually over the phone had wounded Mom's feelings, as well as Dad's, Wootae's, and my own.

During the meal, Mom blew her nose and picked at her food with puffy eyes until we finally got up to go. As we were leaving the restaurant, Dad said several times that he wanted to call the other restaurant, which just made Mom even angrier.

"Dad, what Mom needs right now is to be comforted, not to be avenged!" I said.

"That may be, but how could that guy curse at her over one little mistake?"

"You need to pay more attention to what Mom is saying. Why are you so fixated on chewing that guy out?"

I was trying to convince Dad not to call, like Mom told him. What Mom wanted was to be comforted.

That was when Wootae, who was next to us, jumped into the conversation.

"You're both being immature! Mom, I'm here for you! Hang in there!"

Dad and I glanced at each other and then followed after Mom.

I've heard that a single word is powerful enough to both save or take a life. What happened today showed me that words are not only a tool of self-expression, but also a weapon sharper than any knife that can wound someone's feelings.

Mom's feelings got hurt today. But she told us that everyone has the power to feel better on their own. Then, with some effort, she smiled.

There aren't a lot of grown-ups who will go easy on a kid who messes up. But I guess that grown-ups who mess up don't have it very easy either.

I wish people would make a greater effort to understand each other. That way there would be fewer arguments and less hatred.

If you want to be good at speaking, I think the first step is learning how to control your emotions.

I Am Happy

Date: November 9, 2020

Here's what I thought when my eyes popped open this morning and I looked at the ceiling:

I'm just happy to be alive.

I'm just happy to be breathing.

I'm happy to have somebody beside me.

I'm happy that we can laugh together, and I'm happy that we can cry together.

I'm happy that my hands do what I want them to do, and I'm happy that my feet take me where I want to go.

I'm happy that I get to gaze upon such a beautiful world, and I'm happy that I get to listen to music that magically soothes my soul.

I'm happy that the sky I see when I lie on my back is always watching over me, and I'm happy to be reminded of the wind that whips my hair around when I sprint.

I'm happy that one small flower lends an ear to my stories, and I'm happy that I can dance when I'm caught in a refreshing downpour.

I'm happy.

People Who Show You What Happiness Is

Date: November 20, 2020

I visited the market that Mom said she'd gone to every morning when she was a kid. Our school trip this year was to Mom and Dad's hometown. We rose early in the morning, got dressed, and left the house. There was something different about the smell of the early morning air. As we drove, the fresh breeze from the window totally woke me up.

Since we were hungry, Mom whisked us off to have her favorite kongguk (bean soup), despite the early hour. Smoke was rising from a tiny restaurant barely the size of a wagon or wheelbarrow.

Mom was delighted at the prospect of having some kongguk. We each had a bowl of that delicious soup. Mom had sometimes talked about how much she missed the dish, which wasn't sold anywhere else, so I was familiar with it, even though I'd never tried it before.

With our bellies full of kongguk, we got up and turned to go when we saw the old woman frying up some buchimgae (savory pancakes) on the cauldron lid in sizzling oil. She flipped each one over several times.

Mom really wanted to buy some buchimgae, more because she felt sorry for the hard-working woman than because she was hungry. So we sat back down, as if we hadn't already had our fill of soup.

Actually, I wasn't expecting much, since I wasn't sure I could handle greasy fritters so early in the morning. I suppose I was sitting there with no expression on my face.

But when the woman served up a plate of buchimgae, Mom tore off a bite, dipped it in the soy sauce, and popped it into my mouth.

"Wow!" I said in surprise.

The buchimgae looked the same as any other, but it was really tasty. My siblings and I ate seven of them on the spot, and we got 10 more to go.

Even more surprisingly, the woman was only charging 1,000 won per buchimgae. At that price, I doubted she could make much money, no matter how many customers came... and she didn't seem to be getting many customers to begin with.

While I'm still learning about money, I'm pretty sure that 1,000 won is a cheap price for one buchimgae. But that didn't seem very important to the old woman.

As she watched us enjoy her buchimgae, she kept making satisfied comments. "Want me to fry up some more?" "Have your fill." "My, what a lovely family."

My heart melted before her wrinkled eyes, which curved up like quarter moons. Her eyes seemed to show that she'd reconciled herself with all the trials of her life. I thought to myself that the word "beautiful" must have been made with that woman's smile in mind.

When we went into the market, a lady who was selling baskets of ripe persimmons was loudly proclaiming how good her fruit tasted, so we walked over to take a look.

I guess we were all imagining how good the persimmons must be.

No sooner had Mom asked for 5,000 won worth of persimmons than the lady began to nimbly fill a black plastic bag with a generous portion of the fruit. You wouldn't believe we could have bought so many for just 5,000 won. But the lady just said, "I gave you a lot. Make sure the kids have plenty!"

Taken aback, Mom just said the lady had given us an embarrassing amount of fruit and wished her luck in selling fruit to other customers.

I saw a number of things at the market where Mom used to go every morning in her hometown. Some of them were things that can't be seen anywhere else.

The people I saw in the market weren't working to make money. They were working to enjoy their lives, with the knowledge that doing things for other people is worth more than making money.

I could tell that the old women at the market were more worried about helping out their neighbors when business was bad than about selling more than their neighbors. The women always wanted to treat their guests like family and throw in some extra food or items for them.

They were so warmhearted and heartwarming that it made me want to treat other people like that, too.

It felt so great to run into people who can show you what it means to live a happy life. It was easy to hear the sounds of happy lives in the market. These are the feelings that help us share what we need with others and fill in the gaps in their hearts. They're the feelings that make each day's work enjoyable and rewarding.

There was a lot for me to learn today. It was a day when I was thankful for everything.

They were working to enjoy their lives, with the knowledge that doing things for other people is worth more than making money.

I Am Who I Am

Date: December 23, 2020

I like Freddie Mercury. Why??

I've never seen another person with a personality as distinct as his. He shows himself off proudly.

These days, I'm really into Queen songs. I can see colors by simply listening to them. I can see pictures. My feelings swell simply from listening to the songs.

I don't know much about music, but I like it. How dull life would be if we didn't have music. I don't even want to imagine it.

Today, even the sky I'm looking up at has personality!

218

Santa Claus

Date: December 30, 2020

When I'm struggling or upset, or when my heart is rocking and shaking, I think about Santa Claus, and a smile returns to my face.

Around this time every year, he comes to me without a sound when I'm asleep. He always gives me a big hug before leaving. In that moment, I can feel his fiery heart with my whole body, as if I'm watching a flame burning brightly. That's when Santa Claus slips the kindest love in the world into my heart.

But people I know generally don't believe in Santa Claus. That's probably because he's invisible.

Even my older cousin doesn't believe in Santa Claus. When I say it feels like Santa Claus has given my heart a big hug even though—or because—he's invisible, my cousin tells me that he's a lie, that even the song that goes, "You better not cry," was made up by adults to keep children from crying.

I tell him that Santa really gives us Christmas presents, but he says they're actually from Mom and Dad and asks whether I have evidence for my beliefs. Hearing such words makes me disappointed and a little scared. I'm scared that I won't be able to keep believing.

I've heard stories about Santa Claus since I was young, and I've received presents from him every year. Ever since I grew up a little and learned to read, Santa has been sending me letters as well.

He's helped me overcome my shortcomings. He gave me the present of "courage" one year and the present of "willpower" last year. A few days ago, he gave me the present of "kindness."

But in his letter, Santa wrote that he can only guide me towards realizing all these presents if I first make the effort in my heart. So I put those presents into practice, and every year, Santa's presents give me a lot of strength.

Santa's presents help me mature over the course of a year. This is probably why I always look forward to Christmas and miss Santa Claus.

Mom says that when she was seven, she was in the kindergarten yard all by herself when she saw Santa Claus riding his sled beyond the kindergarten's walls. It happened so fast that when she looked again, he was gone. Mom said she never saw him again.

They say that those with the kindest heart can see everything that's real in the world. I want to see Santa Claus. But I think I have too many things to feel sorry about and too many improper thoughts for my heart be so kind.

So I need a little bit of time. Someday I will meet Santa, and when that happens, I'll be the one to give him a big hug. I'm reminded of some lines from a Christmas movie I saw.

"When the sun goes down, you believe it will rise again, don't you? When you can't see the sun because it's behind the clouds, don't you still believe it's out there? Just keep believing like that. Believe that I'm always inside you…"